Emmy Nation

MISTRESS OF DISGUISE

L. Davis Munro

Publisher's Note: This is a work of fiction. Names, characters, places, and incidents are a product of the author's imagination. Locales and public names are sometimes used for atmospheric purposes. Any resemblance to actual people, living or dead, or to businesses, companies, events, institutions, or locales is completely coincidental.

Book Layout ©2017 BookDesignTemplates.com

ISBN 13: 9781730970115

KDP Direct Publishing

North Charleston, South Carolina

For Steve

· PROLOGUE ·

THE MOON CAN BE tricky. At times, it seems as though
she is never there when you need her and always there
when you don't. Tonight, however, she has a sly smile, just
bright enough to guide the way, but dim enough to hide
three women sneaking in the dark. The moon shares their
secret and does her best to keep them hidden.

The women are dressed identically. They wear all
black. Long skirts that reach to their ankles and tailored
jackets over high-collared blouses. They wear hats with
veils pulled down over their faces. They are roughly the
same height.

This is all purposeful. In fact, Emmy Nation had so-
licited the services of a famous actress and her wardrobe
mistress to help them assemble their disguises. The tailored skirt suits they wear are borrowed from a new play
that is running in London's West End. They are the costumes of the governesses, and were chosen to keep the
identities of these women hidden while they blend into
the night.

All of this is because one of these three women is a convicted criminal and is being actively pursued by Scotland Yard.

Marion Campbell is wanted for Defacement of Private Property. Specifically, she had used acid to burn the words "Votes for Women" in the grass of a golf course often used by prominent British politicians. She had managed to get all but the last letter completed before the police arrived on the scene. It was quite the effort. After all, "Votes for Women", the most popular suffrage slogan, has thirteen letters in it. If you were the suspicious sort, you might choose to leave the last letter off anyways. Surely everyone would understand what was meant if Miss Campbell had intentionally only written, "Votes for Wome".

A feather flutters free from Marion's hat and she watches as it drifts towards the two uniformed constables standing on guard in front of her home.

"Sshh," Emmy instructs before Marion can even speak the curse word she is thinking. "Stay absolutely still," she adds, while bringing a protective arm to Marion's shoulders and pressing her against the brick wall. The three black-clad figures stand still while one constable glances at the feather and then peers into the darkness of the alleyway from where it appeared. It seems to Marion that he is looking right at her, and she holds her breath in an effort to contain all movementt, sound, and panic. But he turns away, clearly feeling satisfied that nothing is hiding in the shadows.

"That was close," Edith Emerson, Marion's other protector, whispers. "Come along, Miss Campbell, we shouldn't linger here. The more distance we have between ourselves and those coppers, the better."

Edith leads the way through the alley, in the opposite direction of the police. She keeps one hand on the wall to guide her in the dark, and picks her way elegantly between the wash pails and garbage bins that line the alley. Marion follows suit, but her feet are not steady beneath her. Unlike Emmy and Edith, Marion has no experience evading the police on eerie nights.

She had been arrested on the golf course at letter twelve and sent to Holloway Prison to serve a three-month sentence. Marion Campbell had spent fifteen days on the inside before she was released due to her failing health. She had chosen to hunger strike, along with almost every other suffragette who had been arrested, in protest of the mistreatment of the women's rights activists in jail. After fifteen days with nothing but water, Miss Campbell was so weak and ill that the Warden released her under the Cat and Mouse Act. Under this new law, the police had the right to rearrest Miss Campbell as soon as she had recovered her health, and to return her to Holloway to serve out the remainder of her sentence. In the recent history of the Cat and Mouse Act, not a single suffragette had volunteered to return.

So it is that Marion Campbell finds herself flanked by two women dressed to look just like her, on an evening in May, with a sly moon shining down, and two police officers waiting to rearrest her. Miss Nation and Mrs. Emerson had been assigned by the WSPU to smuggle Marion out of London, and out of the hands of the Metropolitan Police.

The plan is to sneak away silently under the cover of night, but Marion's health has not fully recovered and her legs still feel shaky beneath her. She stumbles along the uneven cobblestones more than she wants to let on to her protectors, and her body betrays her as she catches the toe of her boot and cannot right herself smoothly. She bangs into a pail of water left out by a serving woman from the day's laundry. It smacks against the brick wall and water spills down the alley towards the constables.

"Bugger," Emmy swears, as a lantern light shines into her eyes from the street, a police officer outlined behind it in an ominous silhouette. "Go to plan B, ladies. Run!"

Edith hoists Marion up and back on her feet. "Miss Campbell," she grabs her face in two firm hands. "Do you remember plan B? Run as fast as you can towards the square, then make your way to Victoria Station. We will meet you there. Now go—fast!"

Edith pushes Marion forward before she darts off in the opposite direction. Emmy is already gone, with one constable chasing her.

The remaining constable stands still for a moment, not sure which woman to follow. Only one of them is a criminal. Not wanting to waste too much time pondering, he makes a choice and begins his pursuit.

Marion runs, as fast as she can manage on her shaky legs. She has only been back to eating solid foods for a week. Not nearly enough time to develop strong muscles again. Yet, with the thought of returning to one of the dank, lonely cells at Holloway with nothing but her empty stomach and doubts to keep her company, Marion finds the strength to run a good deal faster than she thought possible. She twists and turns, down alleyways and streets. She runs in circles, attempting to shake anyone who may or may not be following her. She sprints all the way to the square before turning back and realizing she had not been chosen by the constable as the woman to chase. He must have gone after Edith.

It is late and the streets are empty and quiet. Too quiet, Marion thinks. She hesitates for a moment, looking around her for a sign of Emmy or Edith, or even one of the police officers, but she sees no one. This makes her more nervous than she had been all night.

Marion presses forward, towards Victoria Station, where she is supposed to get on a train going to a place in the country. There, she will be hidden from the police until they forget about her or forgive her sentence. Marion had not been informed of the specific location.

"A precaution," Emmy had told her, "in case the police catch you and question you."

Marion becomes intensely aware of how loud her shoes sound. The heels of her boots click along the silent street, echoing off dark buildings. It seems as if they are calling out to anyone in the surrounding area, "Here I am, come and find me." Marion walks fast now, but suppresses her desire to run, instead stepping carefully and as quietly as she can.

Just two more blocks and she will be at the train station.

Out of the corner of her eye, Marion sees the flash of movement before she hears Edith's voice yelling from down the street.

"Keep moving!" Edith calls to her twin figure. The constable who had followed Edith is still behind her, closing in. She was not able to shake him, no matter what tactics she used. Edith needs speed. She barrels towards Marion at full force, not noticing Emmy standing between two buildings. She does not turn back when Emmy's small wooden club emerges unrepentantly from the shadows just as the police uniform comes into view. The constable doubles over with the blow to his abdomen and curses on his way down.

"Bloody suffragette!" he screams to Emmy, who decides to give him another blow for safety. This time she aims for the groin and is met with a breathless yelp.

"It really is best, Constable, if you do not follow us. We'd be ever so grateful," Emmy says with a smile.

Edith finally stops running and turns back to see Emmy pocket her club beneath her skirts.

"Let's get to the station, ladies." Emmy takes the lead.

"Where is the other one?" Edith asks.

"I lost him ages ago. But let's get on this train," Emmy says, "before he catches up."

The three women enter the empty train station. It would have been wiser, Marion thinks, to have done this during the day, when Victoria Station was full of people going in every which direction. They could have lost themselves in the crowd. Instead they are some of the only people waiting on the platform, and dressed as if they were in mourning. Not exactly what Marion would describe as inconspicuous. Of course, the plan had been to use the cover of darkness to sneak away completely undetected, which she had foiled with her crashing fall. Instead, this is all plan B, which means it is essentially improvised.

The train arrives before any sign of Scotland Yard, and all three women exhale a breath they had not realized they were holding in.

"Come on, the last leg of our trip awaits." Emmy tries to sound chipper as the chug of the train slows down along with the pace of their hearts.

"Oh, I do love trains," Edith giggles. "I hardly ever get to ride on one."

She swings herself up with a show of bravado as soon as the train comes to a stop. Emmy follows her on board, shaking her head in mock disapproval.

Marion pauses, smiling at her two escorts and their ability to laugh so quickly after being chased by the police. Marion had been in jail for two weeks. She had taken one more to recover from that experience and still had not managed to laugh. In all fairness, laughing had been rather painful after her release. Her empty stomach would cramp, and her dry lips would crack and bleed, if she even attempted it. Luckily, she had not found all that much humour in life following Holloway Prison. *Perhaps,*

Marion thinks as she stands on the empty platform, *now is as good a time to start laughing again as any.*

Edith's head reappears in the train door. She reaches a hand out to Marion with a warm, but slightly mischievous, smile.

"May I help you aboard, m'lady?" she says.

"Thank you, kind sir," Marion plays along, taking the extended hand while beginning to climb onto the train.

"Welcome to the Prison Break Express. We have everything you need to be completely comfortable. May I get you a cup of tea from the dining car?"

"Why yes, plea—" Marion begins to say, but she is interrupted by an unbelievably strong sensation of pain in her hand and the sound of something breaking. She turns to look at her hand and sees the mangled remains of what once was a useful piece of her body. The bones jingle inside the sack of skin and muscle that still surrounds them. Marion sees the face of the police officer looking back at her, a wooden club matching Emmy's in his hand, still held high in readiness for a second blow. But no second blow is needed. Marion staggers back from the train, the hand that was holding onto the rail is useless to her now. Edith still has her by the other hand, not willing to let her go.

"Em," she calls back over her shoulder as Marion's weight pulls her out of the train and back onto the platform.

The constable looks back and forth between the two women. *Which is Marion Campbell*, he wonders to himself, before Edith delivers a sturdy kick to his shin.

"Umph," he manages to stifle his yell of pain as he falls to the ground, swinging his club wildly at Edith as he goes. One rogue swing catches Edith in the knee and brings her down with him.

"Aahhh," Edith yells and clutches at her leg, which has instinctually folded against her body for protection. Emmy jumps from the train to the constable's right side and sends another kick reverberating through his body. While he recovers with the quiet moans of a man trying to hold onto his pride, Emmy peels her partners off the platform and pushes them towards the train.

The whistle blows and the conductor's voice can be heard yelling, "All aboard!" Perhaps he wants to get out of the station before any of the fighting figures board his train. Perhaps he hasn't seen them. It doesn't matter why; the train is leaving and it is leaving fast.

Emmy has Marion under the arms and is dragging her along, despite her protesting groans. Edith limps beside them, her leg aching from where the constable clubbed her. The train begins rolling away and they reach as much of a run as they are going to. Edith makes it and hops on board with her good leg. She reaches out for Marion and pulls, and a scream echoes from the woman as her broken hand is gripped firmly and yanked. But she is on the train, and the train is moving. Emmy alone is left on the platform. Emmy and the constable. She looks back and sees him in pursuit, along with the second police officer finally coming up behind him. The train is moving faster and faster and Emmy picks up her own speed to match. The door of the last car is quickly escaping her reach.

"Hurry!" Edith screams with her body half hanging out of the train. She reaches out again and Emmy can just touch her fingers. Just a little bit more.

"Got you," Edith fully clasps her friend's hand. She begins pulling Emmy towards her, helping her close the gap, when the constable catches up and squeezes Emmy's other wrist. He tugs her in the opposite direction.

"Let her go, you bastard!" Edith screams.

"She is under arrest. You all are," he manages to yell back, despite breathing heavily while trying to keep up with Emmy and the train.

Suddenly a large book soars past Edith's head and lands squarely between the constable's eyes. He is knocked backwards and loosens his grip on Emmy. Edith pulls her onto the train just as the locomotive starts going faster than Emmy can imagine running. Marion's head and arm remain outside the window, her bible having just been thrown with expert aim. Luckily, she had spent more time as a child playing with her older brother than studying the New Testament.

The police officers stand, staring in disbelief as the train chugs away with three smug-faced women looking back at them, a bible splayed open on the platform, and a sly moon shining on their beaten faces.

"Good luck explaining this to the Captain," one constable mumbles.

CHAPTER 1

May 17-18, 1913

EMMY STARES AT THE pile of papers from her father's solicitor. She is amazed at the number of documents and places to sign, and the amount of language that makes no sense. Especially considering her last visit with her father. After years of silence between them, she had finally returned to find her parents living in near destitution in the gardener's cottage on their estate. It was the only building they could afford to keep up after her father had lost nearly all his wealth. Yet, somehow, after his passing, the paper kept coming, despite the brief and matter-of-fact telegram from the lawyer.

Mr. Nation passed, May 5, 1913. Presence required at Nation Manor. Immediately.

Emmy remembers the train ride in infinite detail. The way the clouds had been shaped, the smell of the passenger sitting next to her, the weak cup of tea she drank at the station while she waited for Mae's chauffeur to collect her. But, everything else was a wash of grey, blurring in front of her as her mother and the old lawyer planned the funeral.

The making of arrangements and the ceremony were equally swift. It felt to Emmy that, in a matter of minutes, her father was laid to rest with the finality of the tombstone sealing him in the ground. What came next, however, seemed to stretch forever into her future. The will, land deeds, remaining assets, and more documents that she could barely comprehend had been placed in front of her.

"Your father decided to place you in charge, Miss Nation, after your last visit with him," the lawyer had explained. "It seems that he felt you were quite an accomplished and intelligent young woman and would be better able to understand the complexities of his affairs than your mother."

She didn't have the same confidence.

Emmy spreads her papers out over the entire train bench, while Edith sits opposite her, and Marion sleeps. Emmy and Edith had barely spoken to one another since the raid on the WSPU headquarters that Colin led at the end of April. That night, Emmy had revealed herself to Mrs. Pankhurst and had become a double agent for the

WSPU. And that night, Emmy had written a letter to Edith explaining everything and asking for her forgiveness. Edith had given it, but had been quiet with Emmy ever since, despite Mrs. Pankhurst thrusting them into the task of extricating women from the grips of the police. Edith was still recovering from her own time in Holloway Prison and the dreadful state the hunger strike and force feeding had left her in. Despite her forgiveness, their friendship would take time to rebuild.

So they sit in silence during the train ride. Emmy trying to make sense of her father's estate, and Edith holding Marion's broken hand as steady as she can, to avoid the bumps of the train. Marion had fallen into a fretful sleep soon after the train departed, her head resting on Edith's shoulder and Emmy's jacket draped across her lap for warmth.

When the train pulls into the platform, Emmy sees the familiar face of Mae's chauffeur, William, waiting for them. She breathes a sigh of relief. She is home and there are no police in sight.

"Marion, it is time to get up. We have arrived," Emmy says in soothing tones.

Edith helps Marion stand and disembark. Emmy carries Marion's luggage and the small bags that she and Edith had packed for an overnight stay. William relieves

Emmy of the bags once she reaches him and leads the ladies to the motor car for the last leg of their journey.

In the back seat of the car, Emmy's shock lifts and it finally occurs to her how they had managed to escape the police. She bursts out laughing.

"What's so funny?" Edith asks.

"The bible," Emmy manages to get out. After a pause, Edith erupts in laughter as well.

"Oh, my goodness, the bible. Marion, you threw a bible at a police officer's head."

"His face, actually," Marion corrects. "Right between the eyes. He really didn't see it coming," Marion chuckles, finally releasing all her built-up tension.

The three women laugh the rest of the ride, reliving the scene of the dumbfounded constable getting a bible in the face.

Mrs. Nation and Mae are waiting outside of Nation Manor when the motor car arrives.

"Oh dear, oh, my poor dears," Mrs. Nation gasps at the sight of them. Marion's hand is lifelessly cradled in her other arm and Edith limps as she walks towards them. All three ladies are dishevelled, hair falling out of what were once neat and tidy chignons, dark circles highlighting their tired eyes, and their clothes are ripped and covered in dirt.

"Let's get you inside and cleaned up," Mae takes control.

"And go call the doctor," Mrs. Nation directs the chauffeur, who carries the luggage inside and then takes off to fetch the country physician.

Mrs. Nation takes Marion's good arm and helps her get inside the large house. She sits her in a chair by the fire in the library and quickly runs to the kitchen to add water to the kettle for a pot of tea.

Mae, Emmy, and Edith follow.

"What happened, Emmy?" Mae asks in an anxious whisper.

"Scotland Yard has had constables stationed outside Marion's house for days now. We did our best to sneak out under the cover of night, but we were unsuccessful." Emmy leaves out Marion's part in the foiled plan. "We tried to outrun them to the train, but they caught up. We managed to lose them just in time."

"Emmy, I cannot be discovered. Your mother cannot be discovered," Mae grabs her arm in fear.

"Do not worry. The police did not get on the train with us, and we changed trains halfway through the trip. We deliberately went the wrong way and doubled back. Plus, they were not waiting for us here. Which means we lost them for sure. They do not know about this part of the plan." Emmy looks to Edith for confirmation and sees something in her eyes that she can't place. Edith must be spooked. This was her first close run-in with the police since the raid on the WSPU. "Edith, you should go sit with Marion and have a cup of tea. Is your knee in much pain?"

"Yes, but it will mend. Likely just some bruising and nothing more serious than that."

"Good, go relax, we will take care of everything," Emmy insists. Her poor friend, perhaps she has pushed her too far again.

"How are you feeling, Mae?" Emmy changes the topic once Edith has gone to sit with Marion.

"I am fine—ready for this baby to be out of me, though." Mae rubs her large belly. Emmy had discovered her friend was expecting a baby when she returned to her parents' home a month ago to find her father on his deathbed. It was happy news compared to the fate of her parents, and she was glad that she was a part of Mae's life again just in time for the new addition.

"It is more than time; I'm sure it will happen any day now. Don't worry," Emmy reassures again. "Please do not worry. I will make sure your identity remains a secret."

"I trust you, Emmy." Mae smiles.

Emmy carries the luggage from the front door into the rooms they will occupy. The maid, borrowed from Mae's household, helps Emmy as she moves around the large manor, getting things set up for Marion's extended stay.

"Thank you for all your help here, Anna." Emmy smiles at the maid. "It really is wonderful to have the big house in working order again."

"It is hardly what it was, but I am happy to help the WSPU in any way I can, Miss Nation. I think you are doing fine work up in London, but we get little of the fight here in the countryside."

"Your help is most valued."

When William returns with the doctor, Emmy joins everyone in the library to hear the prognosis.

"It seems several fingers are broken. I will have to set them and splint them. It will be painful, and it will take some time to heal."

"Do what you have to do," Marion says bravely, though tears are welling up in her eyes. She is fully alert again, the shock having worn off.

"Here." Emmy pours a glass of brandy and hands it to Marion. "Drink this first."

She downs it in one go and then the doctor, swiftly and without warning, picks up her hand and pops three mangled fingers back into place. It only takes a few seconds, but Marion screams as though she is being tortured. Emmy quickly refills her glass and Marion downs a second snifter of brandy.

"Good, that was good," the doctor reassures. "Now, let me get the splints on and we are done. Keep drinking as much of that as you need." He pulls out the materials he needs from his bag and begins to wrap up Marion's hand in a splint. Emmy makes sure to keep Marion's glass filled, and before she knows it, Marion is quite drunk.

"Thank you, good doctor," Marion slurs to the man when he is done. "I can't feel a thing anymore."

"Glad to hear it," he chuckles warmly. "Mrs. Nation will take good care of you," he adds, as he pulls Mrs. Nation aside to give her instructions for Marion's care.

"Let's get you to bed," Emmy says, helping Marion out of her chair. "Just a few stairs to climb, now."

The following evening, Emmy and Edith are back in London. Emmy stands in front of a long mirror, engulfing herself in an elegant fox-fur coat, the three borrowed governess costumes hanging neatly on a rack beside her. The white of the fur and the opulence of the style highlight her chic black evening dress. Although Emmy's wardrobe has had quite the makeover since Gwen and Scotland Yard had provided her with better attire for her work as an undercover agent with the WSPU, she still feels most comfortable in a plain skirt suit. Tonight, however, she is attending the theatre as the guest of Clifford Marlowe, and he provided the dress she was expected to wear. It itched in terribly inconvenient places.

"That looks fabulous on you, Emmy-darling," declares Alice Sinclair, coming up behind Emmy in the mirror. Alice is one of the most beautiful women Emmy has ever seen. She is tall, with curves in all the right places, even without a corset—although she still wears one to help enhance her figure. Her hair is a rich black and, when it is unpinned, it rolls down her back in voluminous curls. Emmy watches her move back to her makeup table in just her camiknickers, applying rouge to her high cheekbones and red colour to her plump lips. Before they met in person, Emmy often saw Alice in posters for beauty products around London. She is currently the face of a perfume brand whose lavish bottle sits untouched beside her bag of makeup. Alice is not a fan of perfume, but the company had paid her handsomely to be their spokesperson.

"Edith-darling, will you hand me that dress?" Alice asks, making Edith and darling into one word as she always does. Edith passes her a silk dress in an olive-green colour that brings out the deep brown of Alice's eyes.

"That is my favourite costume of yours," Edith exclaims, running her hand over the silk.

"It is lovely, but I am tired of playing Hypatia. I am done with her. Lina is a much better character."

Alice had been performing in George Bernard Shaw's play Misalliance for four weeks now. The production was a huge hit in London. The papers had declared it one of the best productions of the play since it first premiered in 1910, and Alice had been a large part of the ticket sales. Her popularity in London had dramatically increased after her perfume campaign. Her face is in the windows of Harrods, Selfridges, and many other places. That is why Georgia Ann Greenwood invited her to be part of her production, even though they had a notorious and very public disdain for each other.

Georgia Ann Greenwood is one of London's few women theatre producers. She has built her company up slowly and with the support of her famous and generous friends. She has managed to secure the exclusive rental of a theatre on Shaftesbury Avenue, right in the heart of the West End theatres, and she produces popular plays that often feature a big-name actress in them. In this case, Alice Sinclair. That does not mean, however, that Miss

Georgia Ann Greenwood gives them the best part in the play. No, that is always reserved for her own performance. Alice accepted the role of Hypatia, opposite Georgia Ann's portrayal of Lina, simply because she had recently had a bit of a lovers' scandal that was widely publicized and she needed some womanly support in her public image. Although the smaller of the two roles, Lina was a more interesting character and when she appears in Act Two, she steals the show from everyone else, making the lead role of Hypatia pale in comparison. Alice had wanted to play Lina ever since the play had debuted, but she needed to please Georgia Ann at the moment, not ruffle her feathers by fighting for the better role.

Alice Sinclair and Georgia Ann Greenwood are two of the most influential and famous women in London, and Emmy is sitting backstage in their theatre. Emmy is here because of Edith, who was well connected with several actresses, including the marvellous Ellen Terry, who one could argue still surpassed the fame, beauty, talent, and influence of every other actress in England. Edith loved attending the theatre and, because of her passion for the art, her husband had been a consistent patron and financial supporter of several theatre companies. Edith's personal friendships with a handful of actresses had been strong enough to withstand her marital troubles. John

Emerson had not allowed his wife to see her children or to return to the family home in London since he rescued her from the horrors of Holloway Prison, when Edith and Emmy were arrested for breaking into the National Portrait Gallery. Edith was now living in Alice's spare room.

Emmy is also here because of Cliff. When she arrived at his house after her first meeting with Emmeline Pankhurst, she told him a rather big lie. Mrs. Pankhurst had sent her to Cliff with information about a large window-smashing raid on Oxford Street, when in fact the WSPU was planning a bomb campaign along the Thames. Her first task as a double agent. Her second task was to gain his confidence.

Cliff was her boss, but he was also in love with her, which made things a bit prickly for Emmy, to say the least. It also made her job easier in some ways. She didn't have any trouble getting Cliff to trust her on a personal level once she appeared to be reciprocating his feelings. Allowing Cliff to court her was her most valuable tool as a spy.

"Emmy-darling, how is your delightful Mr. Marlowe? Has he asked you to marry him yet?" Alice smiles at Emmy in her mirror.

"I think the real question is, how is your dear, dear Colin?" Edith adds with a hint of schoolgirl mockery. After the trials of the previous evening, Edith had started to warm back up to Emmy.

"You both know perfectly well how they are." Emmy humphs down into a plush armchair. "Colin continues to be awkwardly charming and Cliff continues to be a brute. Cliff, however, is a means to an end, and therefore I shall continue to engage in my relationship with Cliff and leave poor Colin out of it. Although it breaks my heart to do it."

Alice and Edith had only been teasing, but now they see the genuine sadness in Emmy's face.

"This will not go on forever. We will get the vote and then Colin will be waiting for you." But the hopefulness in Edith's words didn't hide the sadness in her voice.

"And you can leave delicious Mr. Marlowe to me," Alice adds to lighten the mood again.

"You are both right," Emmy concedes. "He is rather delicious, but still a brute. And I know this will all pass eventually, it just feels as though the fight has been going on for ages and ages. And another bill rejected in Parliament last week. We just cannot get any traction."

"The Cat and Mouse Act had no trouble passing, though," Edith adds.

"Of course not, darling. Anything that will help those stuffy old men in Parliament keep women down will shoot to the top of the docket every time," Alice says.

Without so much as a knock, Georgia Ann Greenwood bursts through the door. Her dressing gown is a ridiculous combination of orange, yellow, and green with so many feathers around the collar that she can hardly keep them from getting in her mouth as she speaks.

"Five minutes, Alice," she huffs while glancing at Emmy and Edith, who try to contain their laughter. "Emmy, Mr. Marlowe has been asking for you." She storms out, slamming the door behind her.

"She is rather nice. I don't know why you hate her so much," Emmy smiles to Alice once Georgia Ann has gone.

"I know, it really is her deep kindness that comes between us," she teases back. "Emmy, do you want this dress?" Alice pulls out a lovely dress in a deep purple with lace details.

"Yes, please." Emmy's eyes light up. Being responsible for providing many of her own costumes, Alice's wardrobe collection was extensive and ever changing. Since meeting her a few weeks ago, Emmy had not only found a true and deep friendship, but also several luxurious dresses added to her life.

"What is this for?" Edith asks, picking up a black cloak with green embroidery in the image of a cauldron.

"Oh, that old thing." Alice waves it off. "It is from this old actress I met once. She gave me all her costumes when she retired from the stage. I believe that was used for a witch character."

"You have so many clothes!" Emmy exclaims.

"You should see the house," Edith winks.

"I better get to the stage, girls." Alice puts the finishing touches on her makeup, air kisses both women on the cheeks so as not to ruin her lip colour, and rushes out of her dressing room wearing the olive-green dress.

"And I better get to my seat before Cliff gets jealous."

"Well, enjoy the show," Edith sags back into the chair.

"Edith, things will pass for you, too." Emmy crouches in front of her friend, taking her hands. "Like you said, we will win this fight, and then John will realize he has been on the wrong side this whole time and he will apologize to you."

"John, apologize? You are dreaming, Emmy."

"Well, he will let you back home at least. I know this to be true, Edith. You will be with your children again."

"Thank you, Emmy. You are a good friend. Now get back down there and charm Cliff out of his seat. We have a war to win and it will be won over champagne and theatre." Edith raises her glass and Emmy smiles, feeling for the first time that her friend has truly forgiven her.

"See you tomorrow then."

"See you tomorrow."

Emmy sneaks through the hidden passageways that lead to the back of the orchestra section of the theatre. Cliff is looking a bit frantic as he scans the room for her. Emmy easily slips through the crowds of spectators trying to get to their seats as bells chime loudly to indicate the start of the second act.

"There you are." He grabs her arm and, as always, squeezes a little too tightly. Cliff does not like the theatre at all. He views it as a trivial pastime that distracts from important tasks in life. However, Cliff is a politician, and politicians have to be socialites from time to time. So, Emmy has been frequenting the theatre more and more as his guest.

"Sorry. Miss Sinclair invited me to her dressing room. I really cannot refuse that woman; she is very persuasive. Besides, you know that I cannot stand to listen to you discuss politics. Did you talk with Mr. Barclay about your business?"

"Yes, yes, it is all sorted now, he will come to the house tomorrow to sign the contracts. Why don't we just slip out? I've done the business I needed to do here tonight and I cannot bear to sit through any more of this hogwash."

"This hogwash happens to be George Bernard Shaw, one of the most respected playwrights in London. I want to see what happens," Emmy protests.

"Fine, fine, we will stay if that is what you want," Cliff concedes, and then leads her back to their private box. He scowls through the rest of the play, but Emmy doesn't pay any attention. She loves watching the story unfold, and Alice is such a wonderful actress, she can't help but lean forward in her seat. Georgia Ann Greenwood is not bad herself, although Emmy thinks that Alice would be much better in the role of Lina.

"Let's come again on closing night." Emmy smiles up at Cliff after the curtain falls.

"Over my dead body," Cliff grunts back, but Emmy can see a little spark in his eye, just a hint that perhaps she is getting him just where she needs him.

CHAPTER 2

May 19, 1913

COLIN ROLLS EMMY OVER onto her back. He knows she was out late last night. He had stayed up, waiting to hear her arrive in the neighbouring flat. He never could sleep when she went out with Cliff, but that didn't mean he was going to go easy on her. He rolls with her so that he is on top of her, pinning her arms down.

"Bugger," Emmy's head swirls slightly as she hits the mat, and the familiar but unpleasant smell of sweat fills her nostrils. Perhaps a bit too much champagne last night. Especially if she is going to continue to wake up at the most unnatural hour of six in the morning. She looks up at Colin, who is smiling rather sadistically down at her.

"Rough night?" he asks, tightening his grip on her wrists.

"Actually, it was quite nice, thank you," Emmy says, taking the time to feel his rough hands on her bare skin before she swings her legs up and over him, easily throwing him off her as she gets up to her feet. "But, why exactly do we have to train this early in the morning? I believe we could fit it in over lunch, or even at seven instead of six? Honestly, Colin, six in the morning is not a real time of day. It is still night."

"The sun is up." Colin pulls himself upright.

"The sun is getting up," Emmy corrects.

"Fine, the sun is getting up, and you are getting quite good at jujitsu," Colin tries to get her guard down with a compliment before he attacks again.

"And you are getting quite mean as an instructor," Emmy counters his advance and knocks his feet out from under him. Colin lands face first on the mat and takes no time to use his lower position to knock Emmy down as well. She quickly turns her fall into a defence move, ending with Colin's arm twisted behind his back.

"Good, at which point you would...?"

"At which point I would continue twisting until your arm was dislocated." Emmy smiles. "But you never let me practice that part."

"Let's get cleaned up, you have to catch a train by eight, remember? You have that meeting about your father's house."

"Bugger, I forgot about that. Colin, you are a saint." Emmy releases him and reaches for a towel to wipe off her sweaty forehead.

"Where were you last night?" Colin ventures to ask. He knows Emmy was with Cliff, but she won't admit to it. Instead she will make something up about being with Edith or visiting with friends. But, it is Colin's job to keep his eye on Emmy, that is what brought them together in the first place, and he knows when she lies.

"I was at the theatre with Edith and Alice. Edith and I watched the play." Emmy tries to sound as nonchalant as possible whenever she is lying to Colin. She hates doing it, but she also hates seeing his face when she says she was with Cliff. Ever since Cliff rescued Emmy from Holloway Prison, things had been different between her and Colin. With the distance of time, Emmy has come to understand that Colin was not the reason she was arrested, but she still regrets many of her choices from that night. Cliff taking her home and nursing her back to health showed Emmy that he was more than what she had thought when she rejected his marriage proposal two years earlier. He had seemed like a hard, angry man who had no feelings for her whatsoever, but he had shown her otherwise as he helped her regain her strength after the hunger strike. From then on, they had become closer, which left little time for Colin in her life, outside of work and their daily jujitsu training. At least, that is how Emmy wants it to seem. Colin cannot find out about her switch to working for the WSPU, instead of against them.

"Was it a good play?" Colin inquires.

"It was great! Alice is a really wonderful actress. I could watch her every night."

"Sounds nice." Colin had never been to the theatre. It isn't an expense that he deems necessary with his meagre salary. His brow crinkles slightly as he realizes that evenings at the theatre are yet another thing that he can never give to Emmy.

"Well, I better get to the train station. Thanks for everything, Colin. I mean it." Emmy touches his shoulder gently and feels the usual heat travel through her arm to her cheeks.

"You're welcome." Colin reaches up and touches her hand.

"Sorry." Emmy pulls away, her cheeks now bright red with embarrassment. "I just... I better go."

"Go on then. I can clean up here." Colin turns to find his own towel, his cheeks turning a matching red to Emmy's. "See you tonight?"

"Yes, tonight."

As soon as Emmy closes the door to the gym behind her, she buries her face in her hands.

"Bugger, bugger, bugger," she whispers to herself.

Emmy loves riding on the train. The gentle chug of it soothes her and gives her the chance to sit quietly and alone, something she rarely does anymore. She has been back to visit her mother several times in the two weeks since her father passed away. She had seen him once, briefly, before he died, and she had forgiven him for banishing her from the house when she had refused to marry Cliff. He had revealed to her that he lost all his money and did not want Emmy to marry just to save him from his mistake, but now it was up to her to help her mother. The trouble was, she did not make enough money to support her mother. This is another reason she is spending more time with Cliff and considering the possibilities that relationship could give her and her mother. Emmy is sure her father is turning in his grave.

Emmy arrives at the station and is greeted by the familiar chauffeur in a black uniform and cap.

"Miss Nation? The motor car is just this way," William indicates for her to turn the corner and takes her overnight bag.

"Emmy!" her childhood friend, Mae, calls to her.

"Mae!" Emmy squeals like a little girl, running into her friend's warm embrace. This was a much nicer occasion to meet her friend than the other night with Marion, hand in shatters, running from the police.

"Come, get inside, the breeze is quite cold today." Mae ushers Emmy inside the motor car and William pulls them away.

"What has been happening in London?" Mae asks.

"Oh, there is not much to tell, life goes on as it does," Emmy tries to brush her friend off, not sure she is ready to reveal her silly love triangle situation to Mae. After all, she is supposed to be a very serious suffragette, working as a double agent using subterfuge to secure the vote. She shouldn't be having these problems.

"Emmy, do you know how boring my life was before you came back? I live in a country estate with a husband who spends most of his time in London doing business and God knows what else. I barely have any friends out here, just acquaintances that stop in for the required social calls. I am desperate for a bit of action and you are my only source."

Emmy takes a breath, deciding how best to tell Mae about her complicated life.

"Well, if you must know, it is terrible Mae—I feel like a horrid, horrid person," she begins.

"Why? What is going on?"

"It's just... I don't know. It doesn't seem as though it should be that important."

"But clearly it is weighing on your mind. Emmy, I am not going to judge you. I never have and I never will. You are my one and only true friend. I want you to tell me your silliest, deepest, darkest secrets. If you can't tell me, who will you tell?"

"Oh, Mae, what would I do without you?"

"I have no idea. Now, tell me everything."

"I am getting more and more assignments from the Women's Social and Political Union that involve misleading Scotland Yard."

"Isn't that a good thing? You are the only person they have on the inside of the Met."

"Yes, it is. The thing is, it means getting closer to Cliff and deceiving Colin."

"Ah, I think I understand now. You are in love with Colin, but you have to pretend to be falling for Cliff in order to get closer to him and be more effective at your double agent work."

"Well, first of all, you make me sound as though I were a spy in the King's Court, which I am not. And, I am not in love with anyone."

"Emmy, just face the facts. You are a spy and you are double-crossing the Metropolitan Police Force using your womanly powers of persuasion over the head of the Anti-Militancy Task Force—a man you also happened to be engaged to briefly and has admitted to you that he still loves you. Meanwhile, the man you are actually in love with, Colin, has to be pushed to the side and deceived on a regular basis so you can get all the information you want out of Cliff, while giving him false information about the WSPU, so the suffragettes have a fighting chance at gaining the right to vote, however slim that chance may be."

"Well, if you want wrap it all up in a neat little package."

"Bugger," Mae smiles at Emmy.

"Bugger, indeed," Emmy smiles back.

They ride in silence for a few minutes. Emmy looks out at the rolling fields, remembering her childhood with Mae. Losing in sprinting races and winning in long-distance running matches, sneaking into places they weren't allowed, and pretending to be grown-up ladies married to princes. They had grown up side by side, and after two years of being apart, they have reunited as if nothing had changed. Of course, everything had changed. Mae is married to a rich and powerful man, a distant relation of Cliff's, and is expecting a baby. He isn't a prince, but he certainly is as wealthy as one. Emmy is in the middle of the most muddled life she could have possibly imagined. She is struggling to keep her head above water between rent payments, militant activism, police work, and two men who she didn't want to hurt but had to in order to help the women of the WSPU. The day she witnessed her friend Edith's torture in Holloway, was the day she had decided that her allegiance to the suffragette cause was greater than anything else in her life. Now everything in Emmy's life—Colin, Cliff, and even Mae—was a means to an end. Votes for women or nothing. "Freedom or death," Mrs. Pankhurst had said.

"Ah," Mae winces and places her hand on her stomach.

"What is it?" Emmy panics; she knows nothing about pregnancy or babies.

"It is kicking me again. It has been at it all morning."

"Does it hurt?"

"Not terribly, but sometimes it gets me in a most uncomfortable place."

"Are you ready?"

"The nursery is ready. I'm not sure I will ever be ready for this."

"I think you are. I cannot imagine a better person to be a mother."

Mae smiles and rests her head on Emmy's shoulder, as she used to when they were children. "Tell me about this man you are meeting today?"

"Mrs. Pankhurst recommended him to me. He is a lawyer and he is going to help me sell the manor and buy that little cottage down the way from your house. He is sympathetic to the cause, so he shouldn't be a patronizing old fuddy duddy."

"You have a tendency to think most old men are patronizing old fuddy duddies."

"Well, this one is sure not to be. I hope that it all goes smoothly. Why on earth Father didn't sell the manor when he was destitute is beyond me."

"Perhaps he could not stand to part with it. I remember how much he loved that house."

"Perhaps. I'm glad Mother is not too sentimental about it. I think she will be happy to move out of the gardener's hut and back into a real home, even if it is a small one."

"I will be more than glad to have her nearby, especially once the baby comes. With my parents in France now, Mrs. Nation is the closest thing to a mother I have."

"I believe that is one of the things she is most looking forward to. Your baby will be the grandchild I doubt I will ever be able to give her."

"Don't say that, Emmy. When all this is done, when all this suffragette and undercover business is over, Colin will be waiting for you, and you will move into the cottage with your mother and have lots and lots of babies."

"Funnily enough, you are the second person to say that very thing to me in the past twenty-four hours," Emmy smiles sadly. Her faith that the whole undercover suffragette business will one day be over is waning. This could be the rest of her life, despite what everyone around her believes. And if they do get the vote, then what? It is one of the great unspoken truths amongst everyone fighting for women's suffrage. The vote is only the first step. No one dares to mention what happens after.

The motor car eases to a stop and Mae sits up again. The chauffeur opens the door and holds his hand out to Mae.

"We have arrived, Madam."

"Thank you, William," Mae wiggles awkwardly out of the motorcar with the assistance of her chauffeur. Emmy climbs out the other door on her own and waves at her mother walking across grass to meet them.

"Emmy, oh, Emmy," she calls out with her arms open wide.

"Mother," Emmy folds her mother into a tender hug.

"How has London been? I want to hear everything. We didn't get a chance to talk the other night. Mae, you look wonderful. How are you feeling?" Mrs. Nation takes Mae into her arms, leaving Emmy to the side.

"Mrs. Nation, I am so excited and relieved that you will be living so close."

"Nothing is finalized, you two," Emmy interrupts. "We have to speak to the lawyer first."

"Yes, yes, of course. When does he arrive?" Mrs. Nation takes both her girls' hands and leads them to the main house.

"He should be here within the hour," Emmy replies. "What is the state of the manor?"

"I have been working very hard, with the help of Mae's household staff, and I believe we have it in prime shape."

"Good, so we are ready to sell it then?"

"Yes, we are ready to sell it and move on with our lives, as independent women."

"Hear, hear!" Emmy cheers. Her mother has really begun to embrace her new life without Mr. Nation. "Shall we go in? I should visit with Miss Campbell first. How is she doing?"

"Very well. The doctor was back yesterday. He says her hand is healing just as it should, and her appetite is growing. Her colour and health seem to be coming back rather quickly, which the doctor says is due to the fresh air of the country and my careful nursing," Mrs. Nation reports with pride.

"I am glad to hear it. Thank you for helping us with this," Emmy smiles at her mother.

"I am happy to help, my dear. My life never allowed for my participation in this fight until now, and I am glad to be of service. Miss Campbell is taking her afternoon rest at the moment. I am sure she will come down when she is ready."

The three ladies enter the large, elegant house. Her mother had certainly returned it to its former glory and it looked the same as the day Emmy left, two years earlier.

"What still needs to be done?" Emmy asks.

"I asked Mae's gardener to bring some flowers for us to arrange. I believe everything else is ready, so I thought we would put some vases around to liven it up a little bit."

"Let's get to it." Emmy smiles. "Sounds fun."

They work in the kitchen downstairs, where the household staff used to make all the Nations' meals. The large table is laid out with piles of flowers from Mae's luscious gardens. The trio work together, making beautiful arrangements and wrapping them in ribbons before choosing vases for them.

"This is quite enjoyable," Mae beams over a full bouquet of white lilacs and pink roses.

"You have an eye for it, Mae," Mrs. Nation adds, scanning the many arrangements Mae has assembled.

"I think I heard a motor just now," Emmy says. "It must be Mr. Scott."

Mr. Scott is a tall, thin man, with grey hair and a tidy manner. He holds a similarly tall, thin, and tidy briefcase and stands outside the house, looking it over from top to bottom. When the ladies emerge from the kitchen, they find him writing careful notes in a small leather-bound notebook.

"Ah, hello." He looks up at them. "I'm Mr. Scott and you must be Mrs. Nation," he extends a hand to Mrs. Nation.

"It is a pleasure to meet you, Mr. Scott. Thank you for coming to look at the house."

"The pleasure is all mine."

"I am Emmy, sir. Mrs. Pankhurst speaks very highly of you."

"Yes, the Pankhurst family and mine go back for some time. Shall we go inside so I may look around?"

"After you," Emmy gestures to the open front door.

Mr. Scott walks around the house, inspecting every corner and writing everything down in his notebook. He doesn't say a word, and Mrs. Nation, Emmy, and Mae follow silently behind him. Everyone seems to be holding their breath, waiting for the response of the lawyer.

Once they have walked the entire house, the kitchen and servants' quarters, the gardens and the gardener's hut, Mr. Scott finally stops and turns towards them.

"It is in good shape and I think we can sell it for a decent price. I already have an interested buyer and I believe he will be very keen once I relay this information."

"That is wonderful, Mr. Scott." Emmy could almost hug the man, she is so elated.

"I shall write to you in London, Miss Nation, once I have more information. At that point, I can arrange to meet with your father's solicitor to work out the particulars."

"Thank you, sir." Emmy escorts him back to the motor car and shakes his hand vigorously. "We are quite indebted to you."

Mr. Scott drives away and, just as children would, the three ladies burst into a fit of laughter and hugs.

"Everything feels better now, doesn't it? As if it will all work out and be a happy ending after all," Mrs. Nation says with a soft smile, capturing the feeling of all of them.

CHAPTER 3

May 21, 1913

THE CHURCH BELLS RING in the distance, filling the dark streets of London with a musical score to contrast its dreariness. The main gate of Holloway Prison creaks open, but no one hears the sound. The street is empty, without a soul in sight to witness the release of a prisoner.

She is held up by two men, each with a shoulder under one of her arms to keep her upright. When they reach the gate, they let her go without ceremony or compassion. Her body is too weak to hold her, so she crumples to the ground. She is, however, aware enough to crumple just on the other side of the gate. She is free now.

The gates slam closed behind her. She has no energy and hardly any muscle left on her bones to take her away from the cold prison. She scans the street for anyone who may help her and sees only emptiness. Clearly the Warden had not bothered to inform any of her relations that she would be released.

It is a long time before she manages to pull herself to her feet. She relies on the strength of the gate and drags herself along the stone wall of Holloway. Her hair is matted and her skin is a pale grey colour, more like a ghost than a woman. She manages to half drag herself and half walk to the street corner, where she sees a light on in a house and she slowly makes her way towards it. She collapses on the steps, unable to sustain the energy it takes to stand. Instead, she crawls, pulling herself up one painful stair at a time, until she reaches the door.

Her faint knock is heard from inside. Almost quiet enough for someone to believe it is nothing but the wind. But it is persistent.

An older, kind-looking man opens the door and finds the tattered, skeletal body of the woman. She smells poor and looks as though she grew up in a workhouse.

"Please, sir," a faint voice comes from the chilled body. "Please help me telephone a friend."

The man is surprised to hear the notes of a woman with some breeding and decides that he'd better help. He knows what has been happening inside the prison that is just down the street. He picks her up easily and carries her inside. Gently, he places her in the chair nearest the fire, wrapping a blanket around her.

"What number shall I call?" the man asks, but she has fallen asleep in the chair. Now that he sees her face clearly, he recognizes her from newspaper photographs. She has been featured in the paper quite a few times for her involvement with the suffragettes. He decides not to wake her. Instead he leaves her alone and heads down the street. He can't access a telephone this late at night, but he knows someone who might be able to make contact with a lady inside the WSPU for him.

A few hours later, another knock comes on his door, this time louder and more confident. The man greets his guests and shows them into the sitting room where the sleeping lady lies.

"I'm sorry to have bothered you, but I didn't know what else to do," he says.

"You did the right thing," General Flora Drummond answers.

"Amelia, darling," Annie Kenney gently nudges the sleeping figure. "It is time to wake up."

"Not yet, please," she mumbles.

"Yes, we need you to wake you up now so we can get you home and back to your own bed."

"I can't," she whispers.

"Can you carry her to our motor car?" Mrs. Drummond asks.

"Of course. She hardly weighs one stone," the man replies.

"Good," Miss Kenney begins to unwrap the blanket.

"You better keep that on her," the man advises. "She will be cold on the drive. You can keep it."

"Thank you," both women say.

"Such generosity is not often felt these days," Miss Kenney adds.

"It is a bloody shame what they are doing to you women in there."

He picks up Amelia with ease and carries her to the motor car waiting on the street. Miss Kenney adjusts the blanket up to Amelia's neck and climbs in beside her, while Mrs. Drummond gets into the driver's seat and starts the motor.

"Thank you for your kindness, sir," Miss Kenney smiles.

"Good luck to you." He closes the door and watches them drive away. Before going back inside, he looks over at the fortress of Holloway and shakes his head.

"A bloody shame," he repeats to himself as he closes his door on the chilly morning air.

The pedals under her feet give her solid footing and propel her forward with each push. The muscles in Emmy's legs contract and relax as they move with each turn of the wheel. She feels strong, the power of her legs moving her forward towards her destination. She feels free, with wind blowing through her hair and pushing her skirts against her legs. It is finally a warm, sunny day and the breeze is a soft brush against her cheeks, turning them red with the effort and thrill of riding the bicycle Colin gave her. It is exhilarating to be the one in control, to know that it is she alone who will transport herself from one place to another. It feels powerful, despite the simplicity of the task. When she is on her bike, away from Colin and Cliff and the WSPU, she feels that she is truly her own person. No one can tell her what to do or how to act. No one has any control over her and no one is watching her every move to see if she is a traitor or a friend. Riding her bike is an escape from her day-to-day reality. The reality where she is pretending to be someone who is pretending to be someone else. Sometimes Emmy gets so caught up in the lies she is telling that she feels lost, not sure where the truth begins and the lies end. Is she a spy for Scotland Yard or for the WSPU? Is she in love with

Colin or with Cliff? Is she loyal to Edith or to her mother and Mae? She is all of these things and none of them, and that is the problem. That is why when she rides, she just rides, letting it all go, letting the wind fill her with life and emptiness. Colin is behind her somewhere and so is everything else. It is such freedom to ride her bicycle.

But, freedom cannot last forever and Emmy slows to a stop in front of the stone building in Lincoln's Inn Fields that houses the headquarters of the Women's Social and Political Union. Emmy has always liked this building. It is flanked by two other equally impressive structures, all three with their own unique architecture. The WSPU had installed the motto "Votes for Women" in large letters above the entrance way. From the outside, it gives the feeling of being refined and proper, with sets of tall windows reaching up many stories and ending in two chimneys sticking straight out the top on either end. The grey stone gives Emmy a feeling of lightness and hope, despite the despair that seems to be running through the WSPU since the Cat and Mouse Act came into effect.

"Another day, another lie," Emmy whispers, looking up at the window where she knows Edith is already working.

She stores her bicycle and then heads inside, putting on her best secret spy face of smiles and happiness. It's a casual smile that tells the world life is going well for Emmy Nation and hides the complicated truth that she is deceiving her boss while betraying the man she loves and keeping half-truths from the people she cares the most about. Emmy can get through this just as she got through hunger striking in Holloway, or starting out on her own in London: with determination, hard work, and grace.

"Bloody bugger shit," she cries out.

"What? What's wrong?" Edith looks up from her desk to see Emmy trip over several boxes of newspapers and barely manage to regain her balance.

"Why are there boxes of newspapers just lying around in the middle of the floor? I nearly twisted my bloody ankle," Emmy smooths out her jacket and removes her hat instead of trying to fix it's angle.

"Watch your language, Emmy, we are ladies."

"Sod my languagemy ankle hurts."

"It will be fine in a minute. I thought you were tougher than that, Miss Nation," Edith says with a twinkle in her eye.

"I was just surprised, that's all. I am fine, thank you for your sympathy. But, honestly, is it delivery day or something?"

"Of course it's delivery day," Edith responds. "It happens every week, Emmy, and it is always chaos around here when the newspapers are delivered. You know this. What has gotten into you?"

"I'm just tired, that's all. Let's get to work, shall we?" Emmy had completely forgotten what day of the week it was. Things were getting far too complicated for her liking.

Emmy and Edith spend the day typing the copy for next issue of The Suffragette in their usual set-up with two desks facing each other and each woman desperately trying to stay focused against the other's attempts to induce laughter. In the time that they had been working in this way, Edith was the clear winner and Emmy was the one who always broke down into fits of giggles.

At tea time, Emmy carries over two cups of tea and a plate of biscuits for them to share. She knows that despite Edith's best attempts to keep things light during their work day, she is full of an aching sadness for her children. Emmy catches glimpses of it throughout the day, like now, when Edith sits alone at her desk looking out the window in silence. Emmy stands still for a moment with their tray of tea and biscuits to watch her friend, and her heart breaks for her all over again. Edith discreetly wipes away a stray tear and then puffs up her chest and raises her head up high, as if she were going into battle. Emmy started this double-agent business because she thought it was the best way to end it all and get Edith back to her children. She could see no other way than to prove Edith's husband wrong by getting women the right to vote. Only, she is losing all hope.

"Miss Nation," Miss Kerr calls from her office door.

"Yes?" Emmy replies.

"I need to speak to you. Mrs. Emerson should join us as well."

Emmy nods and walks over to their shared workspace.

"Edith, Miss Kerr wants to see us."

"Mmm?" Edith looks up, still distracted by her thoughts. "Oh, of course, Miss Kerr."

Emmy leaves their tea tray on her desk and follows Edith into the small office at the end of the room. Miss Kerr closes her door after them and sits down at her desk.

"We are having a problem, ladies, and we need some assistance from you. Particularly you, Miss Nation."

"What is the nature of this problem?" Emmy presses.

"It is the Cat and Mouse Act. Amelia Grace Harrison has just been released from Holloway."

"Again? How many times is this now?" Edith asks.

"This is the fourth time she has been incarcerated and released for the same incident."

"Oh, the poor thing" Edith gasps, tears filling her eyes. "How is she still standing?" Memories of her own painful recovery from hunger striking flood Edith's vision.

"Her body has been through the ringer, so to speak. After four hunger strikes and four recoveries in quick succession, we fear that she will not survive another round in prison."

"Agreed. No one can handle that amount of physical torture. What can I do to help? I am sure my mother would be happy to take on another patient," Emmy says.

"Not yet. We don't want to send two women in a row to Mrs. Nation. But, we need to hide her whereabouts from the police. We want you to pass on false information that will send them on a bit of a wild goose chase."

"Sounds wise," Edith comments. "Point them in the opposite direction."

"Exactly what we were thinking. We need to give Miss Harrison enough time to properly recover this time around. They think that just because a woman is walking around outside, she is healthy again and is fine to go back to Holloway."

"Daft buggers, the lot of them," Emmy huffs. She is tired of the Met's policies around the Cat and Mouse Act. She had spoken with Cliff about it on several occasions, but he has not changed his mind about the health parameters a woman needs to meet before she is rearrested.

"When do you need me to do this?" Emmy pushes her anger aside; she has a job to do.

"Tonight, if possible," Miss Kerr responds, handing Emmy an envelope. "This contains the information that we would like you to pass on. For your own safety, we will not divulge the real location of Miss Harrison."

"I will get it done." Emmy stands, determined to do her job without letting her emotions take over. She is angry and tired, but she needs to do a little more pretending. A little more play-acting with Cliff and she can save a women's life.

"Where are you sending the police, if I may ask?" Edith says.

"They will be lead to an old house of Miss Harrison's family. It is empty now, no one has lived in it for years. But, we believe it will seem to Scotland Yard to be a likely place for her to go. It is outside of the city, so they will also have to coordinate with local authorities, which will hopefully slow them down slightly."

"A logical plan, Miss Kerr."

"I have already made plans with Mr. Marlowe for dinner. It will be done tonight," Emmy says.

"Thank you, Miss Nation. We are indebted to you yet again. Now, back to work, ladies," Miss Kerr dismisses them and they return to their desks, a little less giggly then when they had left. The repercussions of the Cat and Mouse Act had that effect.

Emmy looks out the window near her desk, giving her fingers a well-deserved break from all the typing they had done that day, and contemplates her new assignment. The brief reprieve of warm, sunny weather has turned to rain again and the sky is a sea of never-ending grey. There is no sun in sight, only the dark grey clouds rippling past her window, ready to spill out their soggy contents. Somewhere out there, Colin is sitting, watching and waiting. Even though it is the end of May, the rain must be making him cold, and very wet.

"Edith, I need a quick moment to get some fresh air. I'll be right back." Emmy stands, throwing her jacket on.

"In this?" Edith questions.

"I know, I'm just feeling a bit of a headache come on and I need to get out of this office," Emmy lies.

"Do you want some company?"

"No use in both of us getting wet. I'm fine. A minute or two alone will be quite welcome." Emmy turns and heads to the door. Looking back over her shoulder, she quickly sneaks into the kitchenette first, grabbing a scone from the tray Mrs. Davis had brought in that morning.

Outside, Emmy stands in the rain under a small black umbrella, letting Colin see her before she moves towards the alleyway near the WSPU headquarters. They had met here once before, when Sylvia Pankhurst had decided to lead a spontaneous march on Parliament. That was the day Edith was almost trampled and Emmy hit a man in the face to protect her. That was before Holloway, before the betrayals, before things had gotten so out of control.

Colin is already waiting for her when she reaches the alley. He is soaked through, but doesn't shiver as she does.

"What's wrong?" he grunts, as if he is tired of things going wrong and just wants to sit in the rain, alone and peaceful.

"Nothing, I just wanted to bring you a scone. Mrs. Davis made them," Emmy hands over the scone, which she had wrapped in her handkerchief.

"Thank you," Colin takes it, remembering their first night working together. It had been raining that night, too. He had come closer to her than he ever had again, even during their countless hours of jujitsu training.

"Colin," Emmy begins, but doesn't finish.

"Emmy?" he lifts a questioning eyebrow.

"I, uh, I don't know. I wish things were the way they used to be. Before Mrs. Lawrence died."

"Me, too," he takes her hand in his large, warm one. He had never done this before, this simple gesture of holding her hand. It crossed a barrier between them of any sense of appropriate decorum, a barrier they had always danced with but never fully crossed, with the exception of that first night. Emmy's hand is small inside Colin's. It is cold, where his is warm, and it is shaking ever so slightly, where Colin's is steady.

It only lasts a few seconds before they loosen their grip.

"I should be getting back." Emmy blushes and turns away from him.

"Thank you for the scone." He hands her back the handkerchief and watches as she leaves him behind in the alley.

Colin returns to his post on the bench across the street. He thought that after the WSPU raid in April, he was making headway with Marlowe and Scotland Yard and that he might be due for a promotion, but nothing has come of it at all. He led his own mission, something only senior officers do, and was immediately put back on babysitting duties. Not that he minds working with Emmy, of course not. He lives for Emmy and would gladly spend every second of the day with her, but she really doesn't need babysitting anymore. He's taught her enough jujitsu that she can easily defend herself, and she very quickly learned how to be an expert spy. She really is a natural at the clandestine work, and Colin is certain that she would be fine to run the operation without him constantly nearby keeping his eye out for her. They hadn't had an altercation in weeks; ever since she got out of Holloway things had been quiet. So, he had been spending his days in excruciating boredom, sitting outside by himself. Luckily the weather had gotten warmer, but he is desperate for a promotion and a new assignment. However, he had been ignored and passed over time and time again. Almost as though he had been forgotten.

Colin had considered knocking on Marlowe's door at Cannon Row Police Station and putting himself forward as a reliable alternative to the group of detectives he knows to be incompetent, but he always stops himself before he even gets started. Marlowe knows Colin's feelings towards Emmy—he called him out on them the very first time they met—and Colin knows Marlowe's feelings for Emmy, too. He really is in an impossible situation. He can't ask Marlowe for anything because they are in love with the same woman and Marlowe might think of him as a competitor. A lowly competitor that he can easily keep low and squash when needed. But Colin also can't use his relationship with Emmy to manipulate the situation and get Marlowe to give him a promotion to get in Emmy's good books. Colin isn't going to use Emmy that way. So, how is he ever supposed to get ahead?

Colin looks up as the door to the WSPU building opens and a group of women holding stacks of newspapers head out to their respective street corners to promote their message. Why couldn't this be it? Why did they have to go and break the law? Colin could easily get behind the newspaper selling and the marches to Parliament, and the handing out of informative posters. He had helped his own sisters, just this past Christmas, to prepare their banners for the march of the National Union of Women's Suffrage Societies. As a boy, they had taught him to sew, a secret he kept close to his heart. The NUWSS was an organization he could get behind, one that followed legal and peaceful means to achieve the vote. Colin was happy to help his sisters, and if he had any money, he would have donated to the organization himself. But, militancy, law-breaking, and endangering folks, he would never be able to support.

A smile slowly spreads as an idea forms. He is devoted to upholding the law, but maybe these ladies had it right.

Sometimes, rules needed to be bent just a bit, in order to achieve a greater good.

***

Emmy is greeted at the door by Cliff's maid.

"Oh, hello, Lyn. You don't usually answer the door, is everything alright?" Emmy is surprised to see the young woman and not the old butler.

"Sickness, miss. Nasty flu has taken most of the household staff. Seems I am not among the afflicted yet." Lyn keeps her hands neatly folded in front of her. She is a small woman, just barely old enough to be considered a woman at all. She is well mannered, but has a nervous quality to her, as if she is never quite sure she should be where she is or should be doing what she is doing.

"Well, let's hope it stays that way." Emmy hands Lyn her coat, hat, and gloves.

"How are you feeling these days, miss? I mean, are you recovering well from your time in Holloway?"

"Yes, thank you. I am back to normal, although many women are still suffering."

"It is a terrible thing, what they did to your friend, miss. I read a bit of it in that paper those women put out. It sounds dreadful."

Emmy stops short at this. Lyn, the maid of the Head of the Anti-Militancy Task Force, has just revealed her suffragette sympathies, even though she knows that Emmy works for the police against the WSPU.

"Lyn," Emmy begins. "Are you telling me that you read *The Suffragette*?"

"Oh!" Lyn realizes her error. "No, miss, I just happened across one the other day and was curious, that is all."

Perhaps this is an advantage that Emmy can use to her own gains. Someone inside Cliff's house all the time. Lyn can be eyes and ears twenty-four hours a day, every day of the week, whereas Emmy can only get so far with Cliff, regardless of their personal relationship. Lyn can gather gossip from the other household staff and collect personal information well beyond Emmy's reach.

"If you were an avid reader, though," Emmy tiptoes around the subject, "perhaps you may be able to assist me in a small project I have."

"Would it be a small project in relation to the Metropolitan Police, miss?"

"More in relation to those women. Something the Met and Mr. Marlowe do not know about."

"Would it be hurting anyone?"

"No, not at all. Although there would be some risk to yourself. Mainly in terms of your position here."

"I think I see what you are getting at, miss. I thought you were with the police and not the women, though."

"I may not be what I appear, Lyn. You must follow your conscience, but you know where to find me if you decide to join the fight."

"Miss Nation," Cliff appears in the foyer and greets her without a smile. "You look very lovely tonight."

"Thanks to your fashion sensibilities, that is," Emmy responds. Cliff had bought this dress and several others for her over the past few weeks, never once asking her opinion, but just giving them with a note to wear it that evening. His arrogance was beginning to rub her the wrong way, although she could not deny that he was warming up more and more every day and shedding some of his cavalier exterior. Besides, as much as she detested the manner in which it was happening, her wardrobe had never looked so fashionable.

"Please, join me in the sitting room. Unfortunately, most of my staff are sick this evening. I'm afraid that leaves only my cook and Lyn to take care of everything. We may be a bit delayed for dinner."

"Not to worry, I actually have a little business to discuss with you." Emmy turns back to look at Lyn as she is escorted into the sitting room by Cliff's hot hand on the small of her back. Lyn looks back without expression.

They had both revealed information that could damage them, and now they had no choice but to trust each other.

"What is this business?" Cliff asks while pouring himself a drink. Emmy notices that he does not offer her one.

"I have some information about Miss Amelia Grace Harrison."

"You do? We have just released her from Holloway this morning for ill health. What kind of information do you have?"

"I overheard a conversation at the WSPU headquarters this afternoon about her intended travels."

"She is planning to travel in her condition?"

"She intends to retire to an old country house that belongs to her family to recover. I believe she is thinking that some country air may be helpful to her health. She is dreadfully sick after four rounds of this. Cliff, you must give the women more time to regain their health."

"I must do nothing of the sort. The law states..."

"I know what the law states," Emmy interrupts, "but what about a bit of kindness?"

"Wars are not won with kindness, Emmy."

"If you say so," Emmy sighs. They had had this discussion before and it always ended the same way. "Here is the information I gathered. You will find the address of the country house and her travel itinerary. I will see if I can acquire more details." Emmy hands over the envelope with the fake plans.

"This is good, Emmy," Cliff says absently, while reading the contents of the envelope. "This is all we need to keep tabs on Miss Harrison. She is one of the more important suffragettes. We need to keep her down in the public eye to dissuade any followers."

Lyn stumbles slightly as she enters with a tray of tea for Emmy. "Damn, girl," Cliff grunts, "be more careful."

"Are you all right, Lyn?" Emmy asks.

"Yes, miss, forgive me."

"Not at all, Lyn. You seem to be doing a wonderful job at stepping into everyone's shoes. Isn't that right, Cliff?" Emmy glares at him, waiting for a kind response.

"Yes, yes. Just leave the tray and see to dinner." Cliff waves his hand in the general direction of the timid maid.

"Now, getting back to business. We need more information like this, Emmy. We cannot have women leaving the city without any details on where they are going. Our constables on the ground are not sanctioned to board a train with the women they are charged to watch and go on a grand adventure, so we have lost a few of them. This cannot continue to happen."

"Understood."

"You will keep me informed of any information you encounter?"

"Of course. That is my job, remember?" Emmy smiles charmingly. He does not suspect her, and hopefully her little encounter with Lyn will prove fruitful instead of harmful.

"Dinner is served, sir," Lyn quietly interrupts from the doorway.

"Finally. Emmy?" Cliff holds out a hand to her. She takes it and allows him to escort her into the dining room, where they sit at opposite ends of the table from one another. Lyn serves the first course and stands in the corner behind Cliff, directly in Emmy's line of view. It is slightly off-putting to Emmy at first, but then she realizes that Lyn has placed herself in that location on purpose. She is trying to catch Emmy's eye and communicate something to her. Emmy looks and waits. Lyn slowly nods her head. She is in. Emmy nods slightly back, not wanting to attract Cliff's attention, but enough to let Lyn know that she understands. She will have to find a way to communicate with the maid without being detected by Cliff, but now she has an informant on the inside.

Dearest Emmy,

I have such exciting news. Firstly, Mr. Scott's prospective buyer came to look at the house this morning. He seemed very interested and his wife was quite enthusiastic. They are a newly married couple from America who want a summer estate here in England. I got the impression money wasn't an issue. Hopefully, this means we can get the house sold quickly.

Perhaps even more exciting, though, is what happened yesterday. I walked into town to pick up a few things from the store. What I brought home instead is one of the most impulsive and wonderful things I have ever done. The owner of the general store had a basket full of the smallest, softest puppies you could possibly imagine sitting on the counter. When I inquired about them, he informed me that his dog had given birth to this litter the previous week and he was desperate to be rid of them. Then he asked if I wanted to take one home with me. I have to admit, I was taken aback. We had spoken about the idea of me getting a dog, but certainly not in practicalities, only hypotheticals. But, here I was with the option right before me. They could barely open their eyes; how could I possibly say no? I brought one home with me, after buying a considerable amount of supplies from the shopkeeper. Looking back on it, he made quite a bit more money from me because of that puppy. I've named the dog Charlie and he is a precious sweet thing that is being altogether more

*pampered than any dog should be. I hope you come to visit soon
to meet him.*

> *With all my love,*
> *Your Mother*

CHAPTER 4

May 23-26, 1913

Emmy is due for yet another evening with Cliff. He has arranged a dinner party at his home this evening, for some unknown reason, and he insisted Emmy attend. She is not sure why, but she supposes the invitation confirms her relationship with Cliff.

She has been sitting in her dressing gown for close to an hour now, just enjoying a cup of tea before getting dressed. She rarely has an hour to herself anymore and she lets her mind drift towards Colin's door and all the possibilities that lie on the other side of it.

"One day," she reminds herself as she hears a knock on her own door.

Emmy opens the door a crack, keeping her dressing gown covered while her head peeks out.

"Lyn?" she says, surprised to see the petite form of Cliff's maid.

"I've come to bring you this, miss," Lyn thrusts a package towards Emmy, who opens the door fully just in time to catch it.

"What is it?"

"It's from Mr. Marlowe. I believe it is a dress."

"Wonderful, another thing he expects me to wear when I am out with him, I suppose."

"I suppose," Lyn responds, unsure of what that means.

"Why don't you come inside? We can have a cup of tea. You are soaked through."

"Thank you, miss. The rain is coming down heavy today."

Once they are inside with the door closed and the kettle on, Emmy and Lyn sit down at the small table.

"We will need to come up with a way for us to communicate with each other regularly," Emmy begins.

"I have spoken with our laundry woman already," Lyn speaks up confidently. "We send out the laundry once a week and she is the one who showed me her *Suffragette* newspapers, miss. I believe we can trust her to carry messages back and forth. Here is her contact information. She knows to expect you. The only problem is, miss, her husband doesn't know she is involved. So, you have to make sure to meet her when he isn't at home. The timing is laid out in the note, miss." Lyn points at the paper. "Of course, if I can arrange for Mr. Marlowe to send me with the gifts for you, we have a perfect reason to be meeting in person."

"Lyn, you are very clever. This is grand. Now, what I need you to do is pass on any information you may be privy to as a member of Mr. Marlowe's staff. Meetings he has, who he sends letters to, telephone calls he receives. Anything that relates to the suffragettes, or his work, or politics, I want to know about."

"Yes, Miss Nation."

"I am also going to be passing on false information to Mr. Marlowe on a more regular basis. I need to know if he suspects me at all, or if he suspects the information. I will give you details through the laundress, or in person when we can."

"I understand, miss. I can do this. So far, he has not shown any suspicions towards yourself or the information you gave him the other night about that Amelia Grace Harrison's whereabouts. I assume that was false?"

"You assume correctly. Good work. We must cover our tracks well and keep a low profile."

"I understand. I won't let you down, miss."

"Shall we look at this dress?"

"Oh, yes, you should start getting ready for the dinner," Lyn reminds Emmy of the impending party she is due at in nearly an hour.

"He needs to stop giving me things." Emmy takes the box, opening it to reveal a grey dress covered in a sheer layer of grey georgette. Tiny beads shimmer in undulating patterns down the front and back of the dress, giving the illusion of evening waves that you can barely make out in the darkness. The neckline is square with cap sleeves, and the waist pulls in with a ripple of fabric. Emmy pulls it out without expression.

"Oh, miss, it is gorgeous," Lyn exclaims, running her hand along the georgette fabric, delighting in the feel of something so much finer than she is used to touching. "The workmanship is perfect," she adds, taking a closer look at the beading.

"Where is the note?" Emmy hands the dress over to Lyn. She sees it at the bottom of the box and rips the envelope.

Emmy,

Please wear this tonight.

Clifford

"At least he said 'please' this time," Emmy sighs. "Why does his insist on doing this every bloody time?"

"Doing what, miss?"

"Telling me what to wear. What if I wanted to wear something else?"

"Then you should wear something else," Lyn says simply.

"Yes, I know, I know. But I am attempting to appeal to his romantic side. So, I suppose I had better change."

"Do you need help?"

"Please, I always have such a bugger of a time getting into these things on my own. And Colin is no good at it."

"Miss!" Lyn cries out. "Officer Thomas doesn't..." She can't finish the thought. She had overheard Mr. Marlowe discussing the partnership of Miss Emmy and Officer Colin Thomas, and of how they work a bit too closely together.

"Don't worry, it is all decent." Emmy smiles.

Lyn helps Emmy into the dress. It looks lovely on her, complementing her figure and allowing her complexion and eyes to shine against the grey of the dress. How Cliff knows these things is beyond Emmy. The dress fits snugly, requiring a corset underneath, and Emmy pulls the look together with a necklace of sapphires that Cliff had sent over a few days before.

"Lyn, I want to make sure that you are still confident about helping me with Mr. Marlowe? I do not want you to feel pressured in any way," Emmy mentions once she is dressed.

"I have thought about it quite a lot, miss, and, yes, I am very sure. It is a special dress, miss. I should do your hair," Lyn offers, changing the subject.

Emmy sits and allows Lyn to do her hair in a loose style, pinned up in gentle curls.

"You have quite the talent for this, Lyn. You should be a lady's maid, not working in a house with no one but a stubborn, grumpy man."

"Perhaps one day I shall be, miss. Maybe even sooner than later." Lyn smiles knowingly.

"What does that mean?"

"Nothing, miss. We should be going. Mr. Marlowe is expecting you."

On their way out, the ladies run into Colin on the stairs.

"Emmy, you..." Colin stumbles. "I mean, uh you... uh," Colin's voice changes from the initial awe of seeing the most beautiful woman wearing the most exquisite dress, to a quiet sadness because he knows full well what this means. Emmy is spending another evening in the company of Clifford Marlowe, his boss and Emmy's ex-fiancée. Colin suspects that Emmy will soon be leaving their little joint flats to move into a much grander house. If only he could make her see that he was the better choice.

"Thank you, Colin." Emmy saves him from having to say the compliment. "I have a dinner party to attend. I really must be on my way. I cannot be late."

"Of course," Colin calls after her. "Have fun with the boss," he adds after she is out of earshot.

"Emmy, you look very nice," Cliff greets her as Lyn removes her jacket in the foyer.

"Thank you for the dress, but you really need to stop giving me…"

"Nonsense, I enjoy doing it," Cliff interrupts her. "Come into the sitting room. I want to have a private word with you before we go into the party."

"What is the occasion?" Emmy sits in the ornate chair near the fireplace. The dress was gorgeous, but offered no warmth on this damp evening.

"We have apprehended Miss Amelia Grace Harrison and she is back in Holloway," Cliff declares triumphantly.

"What?!" Emmy chokes out. "Was she at the house I sent you to?" she adds, recovering.

"No. I suppose you overheard false information. She was in the opposite direction at a house right here in London."

"She can't have been healthy enough to go back to Holloway," Emmy has a hard time suppressing the shock in her voice. "She has only been out a few days."

"She will be fine; the doctors at Holloway approved her return. Do not worry. Although I would be a bit more careful around the WSPU. Perhaps you were purposefully fed false information. Are you sure you are not suspected of being a spy?"

"I am most positive I am not a suspect," Emmy replies. "I take every precaution. Do you not think I am doing a good job?"

"I think you are doing a wonderful job. I just want you to be extra cautious, as you obviously passed on the wrong information about Miss Harrison."

"Perhaps they had a change of plans. From what I heard, a journey like that to the country would have been most challenging for Miss Harrison, given her state of health. They must have decided against moving her that far at the last moment," Emmy defends herself. Her brain is running wildly though. *How had Scotland Yard discovered Miss Harrison's true hiding place? Did someone tell them? Does the WSPU have a mole? She must report back to Miss Kerr. Maybe Miss Kerr is the mole?*

"Emmy?" Cliff says. "Emmy, are you listening to me?"

"Yes, sorry." Emmy comes back to the room. She can't do anything about it now, so she might as well be fully present here.

"I actually brought you in here to ask you something unrelated to work."

"Yes, of course. Forgive me. What is it?" Emmy looks into his eyes. They have always held a glimmer of what could be with Cliff, some deeper warmth that he rarely let come to the surface of his hard shell.

"Would you like a glass of champagne?" He asks, standing and ringing the bell before she can answer.

"Yes, please, that would be lovely," Emmy replies, confused by Cliff's sudden change of demeanour. Just a moment before, he was confident and professional, now he stands in the corner of the room looking at the door as if he were avoiding making eye contact with her.

"Cliff, you seem a bit off. What is going on?" Emmy goes towards him just as a footman enters with a tray of champagne.

"Ah," Cliff hands Emmy a glass and takes the other. Then he places his hand in his usual place on the small of her back and guides her back into the centre of the sitting room. The footman quietly leaves them alone again and Cliff sits beside her, closer than he normally would.

"Emmy," he begins, almost a bit nervously. "I have really enjoyed getting to know you more and now I think it is time that we were married."

"Pardon?" Emmy almost spits up her champagne, but manages to contain herself.

"I know, I know, we've been here before, but this time it is different. We are working together, we actually know each other, and we have fun together. We are friends now."

"We are?"

"Of course we are. I don't have dinners with Officer Thomas, do I?"

"I suppose not."

"I want you to marry me, Imogen Madeline Nation."

Emmy stands up and finishes her champagne in one unladylike gulp. Her stomach flips. Is this really happening? Is she really in this position again? She feels all the independence she has gained in the past few years rush out of her. Being a wife to Clifford Marlowe would mean being a prisoner. The panic blows through her like a strong gust of wind, but then is gone, and just as suddenly as it left, her independence rushes back to her. She walks to the mantle and steadies herself, taking a deep breath. And then another, clearing her head so she can think this through.

This is unexpected, but also a good thing. She had earned his trust and made her way into his heart, as well as his home. Accepting his proposal would give her full-time access to his thoughts, his work, and more. She could really give the WSPU the best information possible. But now she had Lyn for that. She really did not want to marry Cliff at all. He is nicer, and she has warmed up to his gruff charms, but still, marriage to a man that dictates her whole life as much as he possibly can? The only freedom she has from him is when she goes home or is at the WSPU. Otherwise, she is entirely under his thumb at Scotland Yard and for all the social engagements he invites her to. No, she cannot live like that. She will say no. But, what about her job? If she says no, will he fire her? Then she will be of no use to the suffragettes.

"Bugger," she accidentally says out loud.

"Bugger what?" Cliff asks.

"Sorry, Cliff. I, well, I have to think about it. It is a big decision for me and I was not expecting this at all. I am not prepared to give you an answer just yet. Please give me some time?"

"Of course, you may take as much time as you need." Cliff takes two steps and instantly closes the gap between them. Before she knows what is happening, his arm is around her waist and he is bending towards her. She allows his lips to touch hers, wondering what this kiss will feel like compared to the uncomfortable one they had shared during their first engagement. It lasts only a few seconds. Wet, rough, and tasting of cigars. When he pulls away, Emmy has the impulse to wipe her mouth dry, but resists it out of fear of insulting him.

"Don't take too long," he whispers with a boyish smile.

"Please excuse me, I must freshen up before joining the party." Emmy pulls free of him and rushes out the door.

"Emmy, is that you?" Gwen's high-pitched voice flutters through the drawing room to where Emmy has just entered. She had freshened herself up and tried to regain as much composure as possible before joining the party. But seeing her old friend Gwen does more to return Emmy's complexion to normal than any powder could.

"Gwen? You look marvellous. What are you doing here?" Emmy asks, returning the double-cheeked kiss Gwen gives her.

"Well, Howard and Clifford are working together a lot these days. They spend quite a bit of time coordinating the Prime Minister's schedule with information the police have gathered. They have become fast friends. And, what are you doing here?"

"Oh, well, Mr. Marlowe and I have known each other for a couple of years. Family friends."

"You look like more than family friends to me." Gwen's eyes go to Cliff who is standing where Emmy just entered the room staring at her. "He seems to have his intentions set on a different type of relationship," Gwen giggles.

"Right, that, well, we'll see," Emmy grabs a glass of champagne from a footman and takes an extra-long drink.

"Darling, you do seem to be a bit distraught. Are you all right?"

"Not really," Emmy leans in closer and lowers her voice. "He has just proposed to me and I do not know what to do." Emmy's eyes glance around the room, hoping no one heard. To her relief, Cliff is no longer staring at her. He has been cornered by an older gentleman with a long white beard.

"Oh, my darling. How did you respond?" Gwen takes her friend's hand to stop it from shaking.

"I said I needed time to think about it."

"Good, that's good. Take your time. He is quite the catch, but then, of course, you do have Colin."

"What do you mean?"

"Are you blind, darling? That boy has been in love with you since his first day at the Met."

"Oh, that," Emmy tries to hide her smile. "Well that is a bit of a wrench in it all. I honestly don't know what to do, but more importantly I don't know how I am supposed to get through dinner." Emmy looks around the room, suddenly realizing that this dinner party was likely to announce her engagement to Cliff. This was her engagement party.

"I will make sure you are seated beside me, and we can talk about other things. Our time at Cannon Row perhaps, to take your mind off it."

"Thank you, Gwen."

By the time Emmy makes it home from Cliff's dinner party, her frustration over his proposal had festered into an unquenchable anger. She feels a knot in the middle of her chest that will not ease up. It is as though she were back on that morning, two years ago, when she ran away from Cliff and her home and moved to London.

As soon as Emmy walks through her door, she rips off the hateful dress and throws on her bloomers and jacket. Adding a scarf against the night breeze, she rushes out the door again, before Colin can come knocking, and grabs her bicycle from its resting place on the street. She mounts her trusty steed and takes off, not caring that it is dark outside and that it is hard to see the street in front of her. She just rides and rides, as fast as she can.

The bicycle carries her fast and steady, as it always does. It doesn't seem to mind her angry pedalling or her rough handling. It is sturdy beneath her, nonetheless. It doesn't judge, doesn't complain, and makes no attempt to tell her what to do with her life, as everyone else seems to do. Cliff, Colin, even Mrs. Pankhurst controlled her in so many ways. She thought that having her own home would make her free. She thought that having the right to vote would make her free. She had thought so much and now she wasn't so sure anymore. If she could vote, would it change anything else? Would she no longer be expected to get married, have children, and take care of her husband and home? Would it actually make any difference? Emmy had thought that she was proving her equality to Cliff. Sure, she had been seducing him on purpose, but she had still proven herself a valued asset to the Anti-Militancy Task Force. He clearly had not discovered her double agency, as he hadn't mentioned anything about betrayal or counter measures. He just wanted to marry her and control her, to be able to tell her what to do and how to live her life, like he had wanted to do two years before. He hadn't changed one damn bit, that was clear in the way he kissed her.

Emmy skids to a halt just in time to avoid a horse-drawn cart in front of her. She had been so caught up in her thoughts that she hadn't noticed it until she was almost upon it. The horses whinny and pound their hooves into the gravel road, unable to back up or rear due to their heavy cargo. Emmy had clearly spooked them as much as they had spooked her.

"Whoa," the driver yells to his pair of brown horses. "Whoa, you're good, you're good," he adds in more soothing tones.

"I'm sorry," Emmy drops her bike to the ground and moves closer. "I'm so sorry," she apologizes again.

"That's fine, miss. Are you hurt?" The driver looks down at her tear-streaked face. Emmy had not realized she was crying.

"Oh, no, I am quite fine, thank you."

"It is rather late for a lady such as yourself to be out alone. You best be off home," the man points out.

"Yes, of course," Emmy grits her teeth. Another man telling her what to do. Freedom? No, Emmy doesn't believe the vote will bring her freedom. It is just one small step forwards, that's all.

She gets back on her bike and takes off in the direction of her flat, slower and more aware of her surroundings this time. She needs her friends and her mother at a time like this. She will make a trip home to check on the sale of Nation Manor.

Emmy knocks gently on the door of the gardener's hut. She hadn't told her mother that she might come by. She hadn't wanted to come unless she could bring good news. Emmy had been at Mr. Scott's office all morning signing document after document. The sale of Nation Manor had been finalized and Emmy had signed away her father's last possession. And then Emmy made the biggest purchase of her life. She bought the cottage near Mae's house and she held the papers in her hand to prove it. The Rose Garden Cottage belonged to her, Imogen Madeline Nation. Emmy is a landowner. It had helped take her mind off Cliff's proposal.

The door hesitantly opens a crack and then all the way, once Mrs. Nation sees her daughter.

"This is a surprise! I didn't know you were coming today."

"Sorry to come without warning," Emmy kisses her mother's cheek as she enters, "but I have some news."

"Really? Let me put some tea on." Mrs. Nation bustles over to the kettle, fills it with water, lights the stove, and sets out a tray with two teacups and a plate of biscuits, before returning to Emmy. Obviously, the intrigue of her daughter just showing up at her door saying she had news did not affect Mrs. Nation in the least.

"Are you ready?" Emmy asks.

"Yes, dear," Mrs. Nation replies, sitting down.

"I went to visit Mr. Scott this morning and..." Emmy waits dramatically.

"And?" Mrs. Nation questions without growing excitement.

"And I finalized the sale of our house," Emmy answers.

"That is excellent news, dear." Mrs. Nation stands to attend to the whistling kettle.

"And, I signed all the paperwork," Emmy calls after her mother.

"Good, good," Mrs. Nation calls back from the kitchen, which is just located across the room. "Tea?"

"Yes, please." Emmy snatches a biscuit from the plate as her mother pours her a cup of tea. "I also signed all the paperwork for the Rose Garden Cottage," Emmy smiles.

"Really?" Mrs. Nation finally looks interested.

"Really," Emmy produces a key from her pocket.

"It is ours?"

"It is yours, Mother. Yours and no one else's." Emmy remembers the feeling of freedom she had when she first walked into her very own flat in London just a short time ago. She had never lived alone before then and the independence she gained had been the best thing that had happened to her. She was happy to be able to offer that to her mother now. She hands the key to Mrs. Nation and sits back to enjoy her tea.

"Oh, Emmy, dear, this is marvellous. I could not have asked for anything more. My own home, with a lovely garden to tend to, and Mae just down the way with her new baby. And a bedroom for you to stay in whenever you are able to come visit me from London. You know how to make your mother happy!"

"I am feeling pretty happy myself, at the moment," Emmy admits. "How about we go over and take a look inside?"

"What—now?"

"Why not? Do you have anything else happening today?"

"Well, I was going to do some needlework."

"You shall just have to save it for tomorrow; we are going on a day trip," Emmy declares.

"How shall we get there?" Mrs. Nation looks skeptically at her daughter.

"I have borrowed Mr. Scott's chauffeur for the day. He is waiting outside for us."

"Why didn't you say so? I would have brought him a cup of tea."

"Sorry, I was excited. Are you ready to go?"

"I think I'd better put on something warmer."

"Hurry, I am bursting with excitement," Emmy pleads.

Mrs. Nation retreats to her bedroom, leaving Emmy alone in the only other room in the gardener's hut. She really was proud of herself for working out the sale of the huge manor. Her mother certainly did not need that much house and neither did Emmy. The Rose Garden Cottage was a much better fit for the two of them.

"Ready!" Mrs. Nation chimes. She is wrapped in an old shawl and has placed a narrow-brimmed hat on her head that she has pulled down low enough to cover her ears.

"After you, Madam of the Rose Garden Cottage," Emmy jokes.

The motor car pulls up to the small house and Emmy and Mrs. Nation stare in silence and awe. It is just as lovely as they remembered it. Not big, but no gardener's hut either, the Rose Garden Cottage's stone facade is accented by rose bushes running along the full front of the house. At this time of year, the roses are just beginning to bloom and cover the grey stone in bright, beautiful reds and pinks. A picket fence opens onto a stone walkway that leads to the front door. Gardens frame the walkway on either side. Although the gardens are luscious, they appear desperate for the gentle touch of Mrs. Nation's tender care. The front door is painted a dark blue with a gold knocker in the centre. The window casements are in a matching tone and are currently closed and latched.

The house has been empty for some time, but Mr. Scott had assured Emmy that it was in top condition and ready to move into immediately.

"Shall we go inside, Mother?" Emmy breaks the silence.

"Yes, I suppose we'd better."

The chauffeur helps them step out of the motor car and Emmy lets Mrs. Nation go up the path first. She stops at the door and turns back to Emmy.

"I am nervous, for some reason."

"So was I when I arrived at my first home of my own," Emmy reassures. "We can go inside together."

Mrs. Nation turns the key in the lock and the pair step inside the darkness.

"How about we open the windows and turn on some lamps?" Emmy suggests. "Would you mind helping us," she calls back to the chauffeur. "We would like to light some of these lamps."

"Yes, ma'am," he replies and sets to lighting the lamps that line the walls. Emmy opens the shutters on the windows, allowing sunlight to rush in and fill the space with warmth.

"Perhaps a fire, ma'am?" the chauffeur suggests.

"Yes, please," Emmy agrees, and the chauffeur leaves to find something to build a fire with.

With light, Mrs. Nation and Emmy can see the cottage to its fullest potential. It has been uninhabited for some time and has the feel of it, although it is, as Mr. Scott assured, in good order. The foyer is a decent size, with enough space for the proper greeting of guests and a lovely walnut staircase leading to the second story. To the right of the foyer is a sitting room with a large fireplace and a beautifully carved mantle in the same walnut as the stairs. The window looks out over the garden and the pathway.

"I could certainly make a habit of sitting in this window bench with a cup of tea, just looking out at the garden," Mrs. Nation comments.

"Oh, it is lovely, Mother," Emmy agrees. It is a perfect place for quiet thoughts or reading.

Behind the sitting room is a library. Not a big one, but just big enough to house a wonderful collection of books, a writing desk, and a pair of large armchairs that they could move over from the manor house. Mahogany wood lines the walls in bookshelves that are packed with well-read volumes. The library had been left behind by the previous owners, which suited Mrs. Nation just fine. In this room, Emmy finds a second place ideal for quiet thoughts and reading.

Covering the entire back of the house is the kitchen. Mae has agreed to give up one of her maids to Mrs. Nation, on the provision that she will continue to live where she is and travel in the morning to the Rose Garden Cottage to provide Mrs. Nation with meals and housework for the day. Mrs. Nation will be responsible for anything else outside of the maid's time. Breakfasts and anything after dinner will be up to Mrs. Nation, a fact that she enjoys quite thoroughly. In the past two years, she had become unaccustomed to having servants and was now in the habit of taking care of herself, but Emmy had insisted she have help in the maintenance of a larger house.

Beyond the kitchen, one can enter the large dining room. This covers the full length of the left-hand side of the cottage. It features a long harvest table that is elegantly placed in the centre of the room with a stone fireplace beside it.

"This will be quite lovely for all those dinner parties I intend to throw," Mrs. Nation jokes.

"You never know when you will have a full house," Emmy argues.

"I suppose. Shall we take a peek upstairs?"

"Let's choose your bedroom." Emmy smiles.

The ladies dash up the stairs and find three small bedrooms and one very elegant, if a little rustic, lavatory. They open each door carefully and look inside, finding beds, dressers, vanity tables, armchairs, and other typical bedroom items, but nothing that seems suitable for the lady of the house. However, when they open the door at the end of the hall, they enter a beautiful room that is twice the size of the other bedrooms. The bed is large with a canopy overhead and two ornate wooden tables on either side. A writing desk and chair rest in front of a window overlooking the front garden. Towards the back of the room, a sitting area had been set up with a large armchair, a table, and a lamp. It looks out of a window with a view of the back field and beyond.

"Is that Mae's house?" Emmy says, pointing out the window to a large white manor on the hillside.

"I believe that it is," Mrs. Nation answers, turning back to Emmy, smiling again.

"Well, Mother, what do you think?"

"Honestly?"

"Absolutely." Emmy is worried.

"I think I shall be lonely in a house this big on my own."

"Shall we look into a full-time maid?"

"No, no, I don't want one. I don't need one."

"You will have your dog?"

"Yes, Charlie is so lovely to have around. But, I was actually thinking this would be a perfect respite for more suffragettes like Miss Campbell. I think I would rather like to keep helping, if I can."

"Of course!" Emmy exclaims, excited at her mother's interest in helping the women's cause. "But, if Cliff catches on to us, we must stop immediately. I don't want you to be found out."

"Deal." Mrs. Nation looks around her new home and smiles. "Me and my dog in the Rose Garden Cottage," Mrs. Nation tries on for size.

"It sounds just about right," Emmy adds.

CHAPTER 5

May 27-28, 1913

THE LIGHTS DIM IN the tiny theatre and the curtain slowly rises on a very special evening in support of the WSPU. Emmy and Edith are sitting in some of the best seats in the house, secured for them by Alice and Georgia Ann, who were both about to come on stage.

"I've heard this play is wonderful," Edith whispers to Emmy.

"So have I," Emmy whispers back. "Alice says it is a perfect reply to all the ridiculous arguments against enfranchisement."

"And funny, to boot," Edith adds, as the first performer steps out on stage.

The play commences and the audience immediately erupts into laughter at the opening scene of Cicely Hamilton's *How the Vote Was Won*. It is a parody of the suffrage campaign, where all the women in London go on strike and show up at the house of their closest male relative expecting him to support them. Along with the rest of the audience, Emmy spends the next hour laughing so hard it brings tears to her eyes. It is the best medicine to relieve all the pressure she has been feeling after Cliff's proposal. By the final curtain, Emmy feels as though the weight of the world has been lifted from her shoulders, at least for a moment.

When the curtain rises again, a tall, commanding woman comes out on stage.

"That's Edy Craig," Edith whispers to Emmy. "She's the daughter of Ellen Terry. Remember, the actress we met a month or so ago?"

"How could I forget Ellen Terry? She's the most famous woman in all of England." Emmy smiles.

"Well, this is her daughter. She's also the head of the Pioneer Players, the all-women theatre company, and she directed and produced this play."

"Thank you all so much for coming this evening," Edy Craig begins, her voice smooth and trained to fill the theatre space without a hint of forcing. "We are very grateful for the remarkable talents presented to you on this stage. Miss Hamilton's play is undoubtedly one of the great suffrage plays we have, and it is an honour to produce it with such talented actresses and actors. We are humbled to host this evening's WSPU gathering and invite you to join us for refreshments in the lobby. Members of the cast and crew will be happy to continue the discussion on how we can further use art and theatre to support the campaign for women's enfranchisement. Thank you." Edy takes a small bow before walking into the wings, the lights fading as she does.

Emmy and Edith make their way backstage, as they usually do when Alice is performing. It is much more cramped than Georgia Ann's theatre and they have to squeeze past several technicians and performers.

"Emmy! Edith!" Alice calls out to them, waving them over to her corner of the dressing room.

"You were wonderful, as always." Edith hugs her friend.

"Yes, it is a truly fabulous play," Emmy adds.

"Ladies, ladies," Alice raises her voice above the murmur in the room. "I want you all to meet two of my dear friends, Edith Emerson and Emmy Nation. This is Edy Craig, the producer and director," Alice introduces them.

"A pleasure," Emmy and Edith say in unison.

"Christabel Marshall and Constance Henry," Alice introduces the other actresses in the room.

They all shake hands and congratulate each other on their performances and the turnout of the audience.

"Well, girls," Edy announces, "we had better get out to the lobby and do what we do best. Socialize," she says with a sarcastic grin. She takes Christabel's hand and gives her an intimate kiss on the lips. Emmy hesitates, trying to convince herself that what she just saw was how two friends might kiss, and not lovers.

"Emmy, darling, don't stare," Alice whispers in her ear. "They are deeply in love with each other and we all support them here at the theatre."

"You do?" Emmy asks, shocked. She has never met anyone who loved someone of the same sex, and certainly not anyone who believed it was natural and acceptable.

"Love is love. It is what we all long for and desire the most. To be loved, to be in love, to have someone worship the ground we walk on and accept us for all that we are, the good and the bad. Isn't that why you didn't marry Cliff?"

Was that why Emmy had said no to Cliff two years ago? She supposed so, although at the time she had just thought he was too controlling and cold, she wasn't honestly expecting to be in love with him, despite her romantic hopes that the mysterious man who would ask for her hand would be her soulmate. Was that why she was hesitating to give him an answer now?

"I mean," Alice continues, "deep down, you didn't have those feelings towards him, nor he to you. You might find that some of us actresses, not all of us, but some of us, are quite liberal in our understanding of love. I hope you will be accepting, or, at the least, discreet, in your judgements," Alice adds, without hiding her distaste of having to ask.

"I, well, I…" Emmy doesn't really know what to say. She's never been in this situation before, but Alice put it so clearly. Love is love and it is what Emmy wants the most in the world. To be wanted by someone completely, madly, unintelligently. "But, why not just be friends?" she asks.

"Friends! Emmy, are you serious? Have you ever been in love? You can't just be friends. It is total and complete. You have to have the entirety of that person, not just a portion. If it were me, I wouldn't hesitate, regardless of how dangerous that choice might be. God knows how stressful it is for them to live together. It is the same as we are doing with the WSPU, Emmy. We want the world to see us as naturally equal, even though we have a different physical makeup to men. Edy and Christabel fell in love naturally, even though the world sees them as unnatural because it looks different from what we were taught it should be."

"That all makes sense. It is just so foreign; I feel a bit shocked."

"Tea is also foreign and yet it is accepted here in England as though we were the only natural source of it in the entire world."

"Were you always this progressive?" Emmy scrutinizes her friend, who she is seeing in a new light.

"I suppose I was. When I was a girl, I remember having a very strong sense of wanting to protect everyone and everything around me. I saw the whole world as having feelings and a personality and needing to be free. I would cry a fit if someone cut a flower even, and I've never been able to eat meat. I saw all things as having the right to be, just as they were. I suppose that does make me very progressive."

"I've never thought about any of this. I simply went along with what was expected of me to do and to think. It wasn't until Cliff that I started to question things, and now I find that I am a totally changed person. You are helping me to question even more and challenge what I thought was the right way. It is quite wonderful, to be honest. To see two people in love. I've never been around anyone who actually loved their husband or wife. All the husbands and wives I know are married for very practical reasons. You know, money or business, things like that. They may like each other, but never love."

"That is what friends are for, to make us better people. Now, shall we socialize?"

"Yes, let's. I am fascinated to learn more about this Cicely Hamilton. Her writing is so inspiring. But are you seriously a vegetarian?" Emmy smiles.

The party is understated compared to Georgia Ann's normal spectacles, but it is elegant and graceful in the decor and food. The WSPU members and the cast of the play gather in the orchestra reception area, an intimate space normally reserved for drinks at intermission. A small bar serves as the staging area for the servers to prepare trays of small canapés. Emmy spots one of her favourites, featuring figs and soft cheese. The champagne, as seems to be the drink of all actresses, flows seamlessly, with servers walking amongst the ladies holding a bottle in each hand. Along the walls are framed posters of all the plays that have been performed at this theatre. Emmy recognizes Edy Craig's mother, Ellen Terry, as the lead actress in many of them.

Alice grabs her hand and leads her over to a plain-looking woman deep in conversation with Edith. It isn't that she is not pretty, in fact, Emmy thinks she has quite a striking face, but she wears a plain brown skirt suit, with a white blouse underneath, and a black tie. If Emmy had passed her on the street, she might not have even looked twice, but amongst all the glamorous actresses, she looks more at home with the wallpaper.

"Cicely-darling," Alice sings and the woman looks towards the sparkling voice.

"Miss Sinclair, you were wonderful this evening. Truly a star of the stage."

"Thank you, darling."

"This is our friend, Emmy Nation. This is Cicely Hamilton, the playwright and actress."

"I've read your book, *Marriage as a Trade*." Emmy holds out her hand to Miss Hamilton. "I am a big fan of your writing."

"Thank you," Miss Hamilton shakes Emmy's outstretched hand.

"I loved the play immensely, Miss Hamilton," Emmy adds.

"Thank you. Are you also a member of the suffrage campaign?"

"Yes, that is how we met, actually. I picked up the new kid at a WSPU meeting a few months back," Edith jokes. "She was very green, literally and figuratively."

"I was quite ill at my first meeting," Emmy recalls. "Are you also a member of the WSPU?"

"No, no. I was for a brief time, but I was not a full believer in the militant activities. I do prefer words to deeds, as it were, and not the other way around, as your motto would suggest."

"Of course, your profession offers you a very public stage for the use of words as a weapon for the cause," Edith points out.

"Indeed, and I feel that I am better served in that arena over others. I helped to start the Women Writers' Suffrage League and we often support the WSPU in various activities. I wrote the lyrics to a song only a bit ago."

"Yes, I remember it. It is a lovely song," Emmy adds.

"I am also a very big supporter of the Women's Tax Resistance League. I feel that money is one of the most powerful languages for many men, particularly those at the governing level."

"What do you do in the Tax Resistance League?" Emmy asks.

"We simply refuse to pay our taxes. As my play demonstrates, what is the use of paying taxes to a government we have no say in? That is quite unfair. The premise of the Tax Resistance League is simple. Until we are adequately represented in government, and able to vote for our own representatives, we shall not pay any money to the government."

"A powerful idea, Miss Hamilton," Edith agrees.

"I'd love to come along to a meeting," Emmy says.

"We are having one tomorrow. Meet me here at noon and I shall bring you as my guest. Mrs. Emerson, you are welcome as well."

"Oh, I'm not sure that I can. I actually have some rather large news," Edith turns towards Emmy and Alice. "John is allowing me to move back in," she beams.

"Oh, darling!" Alice grabs her in a hug. "That is wonderful news."

"Edith, I am so very happy for you." Emmy squeezes her friend's hand, feeling a wave of relief rush through her.

"Yes, I am more than excited to be going home to John Jr. and Inez. I miss them so terribly." Edith barely holds in her tears. "It is just that, I've promised to not participate in any suffrage-related activities. I could maybe figure out a way to sneak out of the house during the day to do office work at headquarters, but I don't think I can risk going to meetings or any sort of demonstration. I am afraid this shall be my last night out as a free woman."

"I am sorry to hear it." Miss Hamilton lays a sympathetic hand on Edith's shoulder. "That is one reason I am keen to stay unmarried."

"Yes, I remember your arguments from *Marriage as a Trade*. They were very compelling. Will you stay unmarried, do you think?" Emmy asks, seeing that Edith would prefer the conversation move away from her troubles.

"I believe so. I am satisfied with the income I make and I can't see much of a reason to find a husband to help pay my bills. So, what would be the point?"

"Love?" Emmy questions, the subject on her mind now.

"Love? Hardly ever have I seen a marriage that is based on love. Have you, Mrs. Emerson?"

"It is a very rare situation. My marriage was certainly a business arrangement, as was every other one that I know of."

"Well, there you have it, Miss Nation. My point is proven accurate."

"I do agree with you, but perhaps I shan't give up on love just yet," Emmy answers, deciding that she absolutely cannot marry Cliff.

"Well, if you can find it, girl, take it and hold on to it. Love is a hard resource to come by and it is worth its weight in gold. Excuse me, ladies. I shall see you tomorrow, Miss Nation. It was lovely to meet you." Miss Hamilton smiles to them as she waves to someone across the room.

Miss Hamilton walks briskly and with purpose. Emmy has to practically jog to keep up with her. It seems part of her nature to walk fast, rather than the fact that they are going to be late for the meeting.

"What is the state of the Women's Tax Resistance League these days, Miss Hamilton?" Emmy ventures to ask between deep breaths.

"The state is good. We are all getting quite a lot of attention from the government for not paying. I've had my door knocked on several times this year by the collectors, but unfortunately, I don't own anything for them to confiscate. Princess Sophia on the other hand, well, she always gets things taken from her."

"Like what?" Emmy prods. She had read about Princess Sophia in the newspapers. Always in the socialite sections, Sophia Duleep Singh had been a constant feature at the most lavish parties, and her show dogs were among the highest rated in the country. Emmy had also read in the more radical papers, with sadness and a touch of intrigue, of her family's misfortunes since her father had been forced to abdicate his throne in India and move to England as a child. Although Emmy had always believed herself to be an ardent supporter of the British empire, the more she became invested in the suffrage campaign, the more she began to question things about glorious England, beyond the rights of women.

"One time," Miss Hamilton eagerly offered, "when she refused to pay a fine, they confiscated a diamond ring that was bigger than any I have ever seen, as the payment."

"What happened to it?"

"The government put it up for sale at auction. That is what they do with the confiscated possessions of the Women's Tax Resistance League. We made sure to occupy all the seats in the auction house so no one else could get in, and then we didn't bid on it. Finally, when the auctioneer had gone down to mere pennies of what the ring was worth, Sophia's friend bought it back for her. The sale did very little to pay off the fines owed by Sophia," Miss Hamilton finished, smiling at the wit of their prank.

"That is brilliant," Emmy exclaims. "I have never heard of such undermining of the entire system without resorting to militancy," Emmy adds.

"It was quite a laugh. The auctioneer was at odds with all of us."

"Does that happen a lot to ladies that have something of value to confiscate?" Emmy questions, hesitantly. She had been considering joining the league. If she could save the money from paying her taxes, that could go a long way. But now that she had the money from the sale of Nation Manor and her mother's cottage in her own name, the stakes were maybe too high. What if the government took the Rose Garden Cottage altogether?

"It does. The Women's Tax Resistance League is at once a very safe form of fighting for the right to vote and quite completely one of the most terrifying acts one can commit. Not to downplay what you have done with the WSPU, of course. What I mean is that the government is so deeply dependent on tax money to support itself, that with more and more women refusing to pay, it is losing quite a bit of revenue. And I believe that they take this financial loss quite a bit more seriously than the loss of postboxes. It is a sad but true fact that our world revolves around money and not much else, and the government is the main proponent of this attitude. Without it, they have no power."

"I suppose you are very right, Miss Hamilton," Emmy sighs. "Is that her? Princess Sophia?" Emmy nods towards a marvellous lady cycling towards them. Her outfit is a remarkable piece of couture fashion in a rich emerald green. The jacket is tailored in a long, elegant sweep backwards, allowing easy cycling. Her hat is large-brimmed with a cascade of feathers, and at her neck she wears a brooch that shimmers in the sunlight.

"It is, indeed." Miss Hamilton smiles at Emmy, who is standing with her eyes wide and her mouth hanging. "She will be at the meeting today. I hope you are prepared to meet her."

"I've even been in the room next door to her at the WSPU offices, but I've never gotten a glimpse of her," Emmy's star-struck voice is a bit higher pitched than normal.

"Here she comes, Miss Nation, act normal. You've met famous people before, you surely can meet Sophia without making a fool of yourself."

"Actresses are not princesses," Emmy points out. "No offence, but this is the closest I have come to meeting royalty, and likely the closest I will ever come," she adds.

"None taken, but neither is Sophia, not really anyways. Her father abdicated his throne in India when he was only eleven. Sophia was born here in London and has never lived as a true princess. Although her lifestyle supported by her late godmother, Queen Victoria, might suggest otherwise."

"Her godmother was Queen Victoria? That is close enough to being a real princess for me," Emmy states.

Sophia Duleep Singh comes to a stop in front of the two women.

"Hello, Cicely. Fine day for cycling, is it not?"

"All days are fine days, for you, it would seem. I prefer to walk," Cicely responds. "Allow me to introduce to you, Miss Emmy Nation."

"Pleased to make your acquaintance." Princess Sophia bows her head ever so slightly as she shakes Emmy's hand with a delicate grip in a demure lace glove.

"Emmy is a member of the WSPU. She was responsible for the National Portrait Gallery attack."

"Oh, yes, Emmeline speaks very highly of you," Sophia says with a soft, smooth voice that mirrors the delicacy and luxury of her attire.

"Do you mean Mrs. Pankhurst?" Emmy asks.

"Yes, yes, Emmeline and I are good friends. She is quite fond of you."

"Ladies, shall we go in?" Cicely interrupts the conversation. "We are due to begin any minute now."

"Of course, dearest Cicely. You do keep us on track," Sophia replies with a hand flourish. She dismounts her bicycle elegantly and leans it up against the side of the building.

"Lovely bicycle," Emmy comments. "What kind is it?"

"It is a Columbia Model 41. Do you cycle, Miss Nation?"

"I do. It is one of the purest joys that I have in life. Nothing feels more free than riding down the street with the wind in your hair."

"I am of the same mind, exactly. It is an exhilarating experience and quite liberating. Now, let's go inside and hear the latest news from the Tax Resistance League, shall we?" She smiles at them and then leads the way inside.

CHAPTER 6

May 29-June 1, 1913

Colin waits until Emmy is asleep before going out. He leaves his flat quietly, careful to avoid the creaky floorboards on the landing outside Emmy's door.

He walks all the way to the headquarters of the Women's Social and Political Union. The building is dark, as are all the buildings on the street. It is well on two in the morning, not much happens at this time of night, and Colin doesn't see a soul. Nonetheless, he knows better than to try to break in through the front door.

At the back of the building, he uses a small set of tools to pick the lock. The door pops open in a matter of minutes and Colin walks in casually, as if this were the most natural thing to happen all day.

He lights a small electric torch he brought with him and, careful not to go near too many windows with the light, begins his search of the place. He starts in the private offices of the most high-ranking women.

He searches through desks and stacks of paper, opens every book and folder he can find. Colin is meticulous in his search, but also in his replacement of each item. His goal is to leave no trace of his presence, so everything he picks up has to go back to precisely the position it was in when he arrived. Nothing can be out of place.

He is looking for something to bring back to Marlowe, something that will give him a leg up with the surly commander and help him get noticed as a valuable detective for Scotland Yard and for the Anti-Militancy Task Force. Colin doesn't know what it will be, but he is sure he will recognize it when he discovers it. He has debated with himself for days now, and is still debating while he is searching, but he always comes around to the same answer. He has to bring Marlowe something from his own work as a detective, in order to prove his worth separate from Emmy. He has to have something tangible, some evidence that will make Marlowe respect him enough to assign him a better position. He hates going behind Emmy's back and sneaking around like this, but it has to be done.

Colin uncovers file after file of information that he is sure Marlowe would drool over, but he puts them all back. Since the beginning of his work with Emmy, he has felt a desire to stand up for the women who are fighting for their rights. He even went to a meeting once of the Men's League for Women's Suffrage. He believes women are equal to men and deserve to be seen as such by the government. How could he possibly think otherwise, having grown up with so many sisters? He knows firsthand that his sisters are just as intelligent and just as capable in all areas as he is. And now, having worked with Emmy for several months, he is thoroughly convinced that a woman can do almost anything that a man can do. But, as much as he believes in women's rights, he also believes in the law. He didn't join the Metropolitan Police Force just for a job; it was a calling for him. So, he needs to find some piece of information that doesn't jeopardize lawful protesting, but that focuses in on the women who are breaking the rules.

Almost two hours of careful searching later, Colin comes across the very thing he needs. He takes thorough notes in his pocket pad and then returns the file, detailing several women who are currently in Holloway on hunger strike, to where he found it.

He leaves the same way he entered and uses the small tools to lock the door again. Colin takes a moment to scan the alleyway for any witnesses before he returns to the main road. Still no one in sight, even though it is now four o'clock in the morning. Soon London will begin to bustle with the early morning traffic of labourers and vendors, but Colin has a bit of time to make it safely home without anyone seeing him. Emmy should still be asleep as well. She rarely gets up before seven, unless they are training, and even that is a struggle for her. Colin smiles to himself as he pictures Emmy in the mornings. It is one of his favourite times of day with her, sharing a cup of tea and some breakfast, or practicing jujitsu together. His smile fades quickly, though. He had just endangered the trust that they had together, and he was going to bring this information to Marlowe, an even further betrayal.

Colin takes a deep breath before knocking on Marlowe's office door. The station is bustling with the clicking of typewriters, the ringing of telephones, and everyone talking at the same time. He stands with one ear towards the door, but his face looking out at the people working. He sees a constable who is writing as fast as he can to keep up with the story of an angry man sitting in front of him. Another constable is sweet-talking a secretary who is smiling back at him. And just as he is getting nostalgic for the carefree days of working out of the station instead of being in the field with Emmy, he hears Marlowe from the other side of the door.

"Come in," the voice carries over the drum of noise, and Colin reminds himself to be strong and confident in front of this man who makes him feel inadequate in so many ways.

"What do you want, Thomas?"

"I have discovered some information, sir, that I think may be relevant to the Task Force." Colin stands at attention in front of Marlowe's desk.

"From Miss Nation?"

"No, I discovered this through my own investigation," Colin states, hoping he won't be reprimanded for going outside of his mission and that his gamble will pay off.

"Really?" Marlowe looks up at Colin with narrowed eyes. He doesn't look impressed.

"Yes, sir. I know it was outside of my assigned tasks, but I saw an opportunity and I took it, sir."

"And what did this opportunity lead to?"

"I discovered a file in the offices of the WSPU that details the plans to remove suffragettes from London who have recently been released from Holloway under the Cat and Mouse Act and hide their whereabouts from the police."

"We do not refer to the Prisoners Temporary Discharge for Ill Health Act as the 'Cat and Mouse Act' here, Thomas."

"Yes, sorry, sir."

"What do you mean by removing them from London?"

"The plan seems to indicate that the suffragettes have set up several safe houses outside of London where these women can recover in secret. They are planning various train routes and secret extraction plans for a few key figures who are currently incarcerated at Holloway."

"You took notes of all these plans?"

"Yes, sir. The end locations were not recorded, but the plans for certain train times and stations were."

"Thank you, Thomas. I have a source within the WSPU who may be able to get us more details. This is good intelligence."

"Thank you, sir."

"Type up your findings and have a report on my desk within the hour. We can form a plan of attack using that. We will likely need to add extra constables to guard the ladies' homes and the train stations, once we know more details."

"I will get on it right away, sir."

"Dismissed," Marlowe grunts. Colin closes the door behind him. It wasn't exactly the joyous response he was hoping for, but he did get some acknowledgement of a job well done. Perhaps that is all he can expect from someone as cold as Marlowe. It was a step in the right direction, at the very least.

But, who was this other source in the WSPU? Colin hadn't heard anything about this before. He will have to ask Emmy about it later; right now he had a report to type. Maybe with that in hand, he will be able to ask Marlowe if he can lead the extra men in the operation.

Two days after his report is filed, Colin leads the team charged with guarding Paddington Station, while another team of constables board a train at Victoria Station heading to the countryside. When they arrive in the country, they are met by local authorities in trucks for the remainder of their trip. The trucks drop them down the road, and thirty or so men spill out onto the green gardens surrounding Nation Manor.

Cliff had not believed it when his mole had told him that Emmy's mother, with the assistance of Emmy herself, was providing one of the safe houses Colin had read about. He still didn't quite believe it, even though he had sent in the team to investigate and apprehend anyone who was on site. He did know, however, that Colin should be left out of the whole thing. The boy was too sentimental with Emmy and could not be trusted with the information. If it was true, she could not have any warning. So, he had occupied the boy with exactly what he so desperately wanted, more responsibility in the Met and a small command of his own. Colin had no idea that Cliff had sent anyone to Nation Manor and Cliff had it on good authority that Emmy was at the theatre in London that evening, so everyone should be out of the way of his best team of men.

The unit Cliff has sent to Nation Manor establishes their positions around the house. Men move silently to cover every exit, and more men fan out in a large circle surrounding the property in case one of the suffragettes tries to slip out a window. They all feel a bit ridiculous. Why Marlowe had felt the need to send so many men and treat the situation as if they were the army about to storm a military fort, was beyond them. Even the man in charge, Officer Black, thought the whole operation a bit overboard. Despite the fact that he had his men take up the positions Mr. Marlowe had outlined, Officer Black had every intention of just knocking on the front door and politely telling the women they are being arrested. In Black's opinion, Marlowe was becoming a bit paranoid.

The sun had just set, so there was still a light aura of dusk encircling the stone house along with the uniformed constables. The manor was fairly large, although not as large as some of the old estates in the area. The Nations had been "new money", as it was called, when they had any money at all.

Officer Black spread the word amongst the constables to be alert and on guard. He was going to knock on the door. More than one of the officers, including Black himself, found it curious that despite the sun setting, not a single light was visible from any window.

Black knocks and waits. He is relatively patient. It is a large house and presumably full of sickly women.

He knocks again, louder this time. But still no response. He steps back a bit, looks up towards a window on the second floor, but sees nothing. The house does not appear abandoned on the outside. The gardens and landscaping are immaculate and the windows are cleaner than any Black had ever seen in London. But, it certainly feels like it is abandoned.

Black walks around the house, signalling for the waiting constables hiding behind trees and bushes to stay still. He finds a window low enough to look in and cups his hands around his face as he does. What he sees inside confirms his suspicions. No lights or candles anywhere, all the furniture is covered in white sheets, and not a soul in sight. They will have to break in. Marlowe wants every stone unturned.

Black returns to the group of constables surrounding the front.

"It appears abandoned, but we are going in anyways. You, Jeffers, go around the back and tell Officer Jones that he has my go-ahead to break open the servants' entrance and start a thorough search," Black says, and a young constable takes off at an eager run. "The rest of us are going in the front."

The police break down the doors and swarm inside from both ends of the house. They pour through, quickly and efficiently. Every room is looked in, sheets thrown off furniture, wardrobes opened, and any nook big enough to possibly hide a woman is investigated.

"There is no one here," Officer Jones reports to Black when they meet up in the middle of the house.

"We didn't find any trace of them either," Black replies, sullen. He did not relish the idea of going back to Mr. Marlowe empty-handed.

"I think we have a mole," Emmy whispers to Miss Kerr in her office at the WSPU headquarters.

"Why do you say that?" She looks at Emmy quizzically, as if she is still not sure she believes this woman is on their side.

"My father's old house was raided last night. I just got word from my mother. It is empty, of course. My mother, along with Marion and the two new girls you moved up there the other night, relocated to the Rose Garden Cottage last week, but someone knew about it and told the Yard."

"Perhaps one of the women was followed on her way to Nation Manor."

"It doesn't matter how they found out though, does it? Mr. Marlowe knows that was my family home; he will suspect me now. And if we do have a mole, I will be all the more in danger. I already feel as though someone is looking over my shoulder at every turn."

"What do you suppose we do about it?"

"I'm not sure, at the moment. We could set a trap, but we need some ideas of who the culprit may be. Oh!" Emmy exclaims suddenly, as she comes to a conclusion that she deeply hopes is not the truth.

"What are you thinking?"

"What if it is Colin? He has the easiest access to all of the work that I do. I am careful around him, and always hide any papers, but still. He follows me everywhere I go and he lives next door."

"Do you really think it could be him?"

"He would be doing his job correctly, if it is. So, he is my first suspect. In which case, we cannot set a trap here at the office. It will have to be at home."

"So, we do it at your home. What do you suggest we do?"

Emmy paces the office for a few minutes. Various ideas come to her, but all are too complicated. Finally, she lands on something so simple, it might just work.

"Let's give two pieces of information. One will be in an envelope, let's say it is the location of another suffragette being transported out of the city to recover. But, I will tell Colin a different piece of information. Mislead him. Then we will wait at the location we put in the envelope and see if he turns up."

"Sounds like a plan."

"But, Miss Kerr, we cannot tell a soul about this. Not even Edith will know. Just you and me, that is the only way to confirm if Colin is the mole or not."

"I understand, Miss Nation," Miss Kerr says solemnly. She may not fully trust Emmy Nation, but with Emmy's plan, she will be able to determine if they have a mole or not. If not, perhaps Miss Kerr should turn her attentions towards Miss Nation herself.

❦

"Alice?" Emmy pokes her head around the door of her friend's dressing room.

"Emmy-darling! Come in," Alice smiles at her, wearing a red-haired wig with a large green bow in it. "What are you doing here? I wasn't expecting to see you until later this week."

"I know, I just needed to be around someone I trust."

"What the devil are you talking about?"

"I think Colin might be spying on me and reporting back to Cliff. I think I might have been discovered as being a double agent, and by the one person who I trusted the most."

"Also, the one person you are lying to the most," Alice points out. "I'm sorry. I didn't mean to offend, but if Colin has found you out, perhaps he is as hurt as you are feeling right now. I remember when Edith discovered your allegiance to Scotland Yard. She felt as though a friend had died. It can be hard to learn that your friends are not being honest."

"Boy, do I know. It all stems from my betrayal of every relationship I've ever had. Am I the most selfish person in the world, Alice? I feel like I am. I keep thinking I am doing the right thing, now that my eyes have been opened to the women's cause. That by putting the fight first, I am acting nobly for the good of others. But it seems as though all I do is hurt the people who I care about the most."

"Emmy, I don't know much about this sort of thing. You and Edith are the only true friends I have. This world I live in is all make-believe and showmanship; so many of my friends are superficial and false. But, you and Edith are real. I know that, even though we've only been friends for a short time. If you were to give me up to the police right now for helping you, I trust that your reasons would be of good intent and pure in your belief that the end goal was worth the sacrifice. You have said yourself that Colin is a friend of the suffrage movement. Perhaps not the WSPU, but he believes in women's equality. So regardless of what happens, Colin must think he is also doing the right thing for you and for us all."

"You are right. Of course, you are right. That all makes sense, it just feels so terrible, like I am the snake in the garden."

"You are no snake, Emmy. You are simply a woman who has been thrown into a difficult situation. You have been given a great opportunity through your connections to Scotland Yard and to Clifford Marlowe, but that opportunity will come at a cost. Edith and I, we are here, no matter what happens. Even if we get hurt by you, even if we get angry with you, as long as you are guided by your commitment to women's rights, we will forgive you all things. Perhaps you should afford Colin the same regard."

"Thank you, Alice. You are a true friend and a great comfort to me."

"Now, I have an audience to get to. How do I look?" Alice takes off her robe to reveal the most heinous of costumes. The ankle-length dress is covered in bulbous fabric flowers that have been tacked on in a nonsensical pattern. Every colour seems to be represented, and none of them complement each other. A clump of orange chiffon blooms, that may or may not be roses, is placed at the waist where the fabric has been gathered to create an odd cascading effect down the skirt. Alice looks as if her seamstress opened her basket of fabric scraps and attempted to make the ugliest dress she could out of them.

"Terrible," Emmy laughs.

"Good, that is exactly what the part calls for. I can't wait for Georgia Ann to allow me some of the leads in these productions of hers. I am getting tired of playing the funny sidekick or the bland ingénue."

"You do it so well, though." Emmy hugs her.

"Go be our champion, Emmy Nation. It is up to you to do the most unsavoury of tasks in this fight. Unfair as that may be."

"I will do my best."

Alice leaves Emmy alone in the dressing room. Emmy feels only slightly better. It is a bittersweet realization that she had been given the chance to do the most dirty and lowly of work in this fight, the kind where you betray every person that means something to you. But, Alice is right, she is the only one who can do this. She is the only one with the connections to all sides of the equation, so she has to use them to her advantage and the advantage of women across the country. That is her burden and her gift.

Emmy quietly taps on the window of the servants' common room at Cliff's house. She had been waiting outside all night for Lyn to be alone in the room. Finally, everyone else had gone off to bed or to close up the house for the night, and Lyn had been left to clear their dinner dishes.

She looks up suddenly when Emmy taps the window, with wide, nervous eyes. When she recognizes that it is Emmy, she visibly relaxes and goes to the back door.

"Miss Emmy, what are you doing out here? Why don't you come to the front door?"

"I am not here to see Cliff, just you. I couldn't run the risk of someone else answering. Can you come outside to talk?"

"Just for a moment; I don't want anyone seeing me talking to you out here. They don't pay me much mind, but one little thing I do that is out of the ordinary and I will be suspect number one for everything that happens in here."

"I'll be quick," Emmy assures her, and Lyn steps outside into the moonlight, closing the door behind her.

"The WSPU suspects a mole. Someone other than me working for Scotland Yard. We don't have any clues as to who it is. Have you overheard anything about this from Cliff or the other servants?"

"No, not that I recall."

"Keep your ears open for this in particular, Lyn. We need to find out who it is. Anything that you think might be a conversation about the mole, or that might lead to them, would be invaluable to the cause."

"Understood, Miss Emmy. I will see what I can discover."

"Lyn, are you sure you are still comfortable with this?"

"Comfortable? I've never been comfortable with hardly anything in my life, most of all spying on my boss. But, I still believe it is the right thing to do, if that is what you are asking. And I am still doing it, so don't bother telling me to stop."

"Thank you, Lyn. Best of luck." Emmy gives her a quick hug and dashes away unseen.

June 2, 1913

Dearest Emmy,

My dear daughter, please let me know that you are all right. After the raid of our old home, I am worried sick about you in London with that dreadful man. How grateful I am that you ran away and did not marry him. Please write and let me know what is happening.

It has been a week full of action here. I have the most exciting news; Mae has had her baby. She gave birth to a healthy boy last night just after midnight. I stayed overnight in case she needed me, but everything went very smoothly and she seems to be in good condition. The baby's name is Gregory.

The new women who have arrived are in worse shape than Miss Campbell was. I am returning home today to continue taking charge of their recovery. It is painful to see them struggle so much with eating and drinking. But, Charlie makes everyone feel better. Miss Campbell has made him a toy to play with, and he loves to toss it across the room and dive after it, causing all the women to smile and laugh after him. Since the weather has been nice, they are able to spend a good amount of time sitting outside with him. I believe the fresh air is helping their recovery time significantly.

I enjoy having them here with me and helping the Women's Social and Political Union in any way that I can. Feel free to bring more women here if they need it. I have spoken with the local hospital and they have a few old cots that are not in use anymore. I went to look at them the day before yesterday and, save for a few tears in the fabric, they are in perfect condition. Miss Campbell will help me mend them and then we can set up the library as a makeshift bedroom for a few more ladies.

With love,

Your Mother

CHAPTER 7

June 4-14, 1913

Emmy and Edith are huddled together trying to decipher the messy handwritten editorial of Christabel Pankhurst when the door of the WSPU headquarters bursts open and a woman neither of them has ever seen before rushes in.

"She's dead, call Mrs. Pankhurst, she's dead!" the woman cries.

The office goes completely silent. Everyone stops and stares at this woman, no one daring to ask the obvious question.

"Didn't you hear me?" the woman speaks again, her voice going up an entire octave at the end of the sentence. "Call Mrs. Pankhurst."

"Sally, honey, who is dead?" Miss Kerr says with a soothing voice. She moves towards the woman and reaches out to take her hand in a calming gesture.

"Emily. Emily Davison."

"What? How?" Miss Kerr questions, along with the murmurs of everyone else in the room. Emily Wilding Davison was a well-known name around the WSPU offices. She was one of the more radical members, one who did not put much authority in Mrs. Pankhurst and Christabel, but rather did what she wanted, when she wanted, despite the official stance of the organization.

"Did you know her?" Emmy whispers to Edith.

"No, but I knew of her. I did actually sit beside her one time at a meeting, but I did not speak with her beyond simple pleasantries. Did you ever meet her?"

"Never. I had heard about her as well, but had never seen her."

"Harriet," Miss Kerr says to the first person she sees. "Please go into the office and dial out to Mrs. Pankhurst right away to let her know the sad news." Miss Kerr places a hand on Sally's shoulder and leads her to a chair.

"I wonder what happened. Let's get a bit closer to hear what Sally has to say," Emmy suggests, and she and Edith sidle up as close as they can get to the hysterical woman, amidst the crowd around her.

"We were at the derby, the Epsom Derby, and Emily said she was going to do something big, but she wouldn't say what it was. The race started and we were standing right at the side, in the first row of spectators. We could feel the ground shaking with the pounding of the hooves, that's how close we were. Then they came around the corner, faster than I've ever seen anything move before. Like a train, only animals with men sitting on top. We had seen King George's horse before the race. They had strutted him around, showing him off or getting warmed up, I suppose. So, we knew what horse was his—Anmer, it's called, I think. We knew it was the King's horse and we knew what the jockey looked like. Emily, she saw the horses coming and she saw Anmer coming, too. He was lagging behind, so the leading horses charged past first and then out she went. She just ducked under the barrier and stepped out in front of the horse, arms up, like she was going to throw her scarf around the horse's bridle."

The crowd of women gasp.

"Whatever for?" someone asks.

"I don't know. All I know is that she had a WSPU scarf in her hand. I think she was trying to attach it to him, to Anmer, so he'd be flying the WSPU flag, but she didn't tell me about any of this before, she just went out and did it."

"Oh, my. What happened then?" Miss Kerr prompts.

"Then she went down. She and the horse. It all happened so fast. Emily stepped out in front of the horse and then she was on the ground, the horse too, and the jockey was flying. I heard cracks, it was so loud, the cracks her bones made under the pounding of Anmer's hooves. Maybe she would have been okay, if that was it, but then the horse got up again and he stepped all over her. He was panicked, spooked, and he had no mind to watch where he was stepping. He ran off, dragging that poor jockey behind him. Finally, the foot that was tangled in the stirrup came loose and the jockey was released from the horse that still ran wild. Emily didn't move though. People rushed towards her, me included, and she didn't move. Her body lay so still, her face limp to everything around her. The scarf still in her hand. This scarf. I bent over her, felt for any signs of life. Nothing. I took the scarf and I ran out of there. All the way back to the train and then here. Oh, God, it was terrible. I will have nightmares about it for the rest of my life. I am sure of it."

"How about a cuppa?" Edith offers the poor woman. Sally looks up as if Edith had said the only thing in the world that could comfort her in that moment. Edith goes to put the kettle on and the woman who had made the telephone call came out.

"Mrs. Pankhurst already knew. The newspapers are all over it, since so much press was there for the race. They have already tried to get an interview from her. Apparently, Emily is still alive and at Epsom Cottage Hospital;

her condition is not good, though. A fractured skull and many internal injuries. The jockey, it is said, is likely going to survive."

"And to think I left her there. I left her alone to suffer like that. I thought she was dead, I could have sworn. I checked, I checked her breathing. She wasn't breathing." Sally panics, eyes darting around the room, pleading for the women to believe her.

"Here you go. Don't think about that now, just drink your tea and try to breathe." Edith hands Sally a cup of tea. "You did what you thought you needed to do. I am sure that she appeared to be lifeless, if you say so. I can only imagine how terrible it all looked."

"Thank you." Sally smiles vaguely at Edith.

"Everyone," Miss Kerr speaks to the room. "This is a sad event, but until we know more about Emily's situation, let us continue our work."

The women disperse, all going back to their previous places, but none of them really feeling the same. One of their rank had just jeopardized her life to advance their cause. "Freedom or death," Mrs. Pankhurst had said.

By the eighth of June, Emily Davison was dead and Emmy found herself part of a circle of women arguing over her funeral arrangements in Mrs. Pankhurst's sitting room.

"We shouldn't use her funeral as a propaganda tool," Miss Annie Kenney says. "This is a person we are talking about, not a political move." Despite the comfortable sitting room with lush chairs and a roaring fire, the tension is growing quickly. Mrs. Pankhurst sits close to the flames, wrapped in a shawl, even though this is the warmest day they've had all summer. A painting of her and her husband in younger days hangs above the mantel, reminding Emmy of just how sick Mrs. Pankhurst has become.

"She made herself a martyr when she threw herself under that horse," Mrs. Drummond argues. "I think she would want us to make her into a propaganda tool."

"I agree," Mrs. Pankhurst, who has sat pensively throughout the discussion, finally speaks up. "Emily was one of the most devoted soldiers, much to our annoyance at times. She rarely followed orders, and did things that the WSPU certainly did not approve of. She did all of it because she was an absolute believer in the fight and in militant actions. If anyone would want to be used in the afterlife as a martyr and symbol, I believe it is Emily. Alice, what can the Actresses' Franchise League do for us in the organization of an 'event for the history books', as you suggested?"

"All the support that you need. I met with the organizers yesterday and we are all on the same page here. We are prepared to help you plan a spectacle of a funeral."

"Good, what do you have in mind?"

"We recommend a large funeral procession. We can start at Victoria Station and make our way through the streets to Bloomsbury, and finally to King's Cross. We have a horse-drawn carriage with four white horses pulling it, to hold the coffin, which is to be covered in suffrage banners and surrounded by flowers on all sides. Behind the carriage, in flower-covered motor cars, will be yourselves, members of her family, and any other important people. The members of the Women's Social and Political Union, and any other suffrage organizations, will march behind the motor cars wearing all white. They can hold flowers in their hands and wear their organizations' sashes. Some will hold banners that we will make in Emily's honour. The priest will walk in front of the coffin, along with a few key suffrage figures that we will choose. Her closest friends and some public figures that people will recognize."

"This all sounds good. I will leave it up to you all to put it together. Coordinate with Grace Roe. Emmy?" Mrs. Pankhurst sounds tired when speaking.

"Yes, Mrs. Pankhurst?"

"We will need you to convince Scotland Yard to let this procession happen. It will be a big event, with lots of participants and, I am sure, spectators. We will need police present to keep the peace, but also to allow us to proceed without arrest or hindrance from them."

"I can do that; it won't be a problem."

"Now, ladies, I am afraid I must go lie down. My strength has not yet returned to me from my last visit to Holloway. Please forgive me."

"Of course, Emmeline. Allow me to help you to your bed." Mrs. Drummond assists Mrs. Pankhurst out of the room. The remaining three women watch silently as their formidable leader shivers and stumbles while walking only a short distance. The toll is weighing heavily on her body.

"Ladies, we have our orders," Miss Kenney interrupts the silence. "Let's get to them."

Alice and Emmy leave together, not a word spoken until they are on the street. When they are a safe distance from the house, Emmy speaks up.

"Do you think she will be okay? She looks so frail."

"She will pull through. She has done it before. I believe in her, and I believe that she is doing the right thing."

"Let me know if I can help with the plans at all."

"I will, but for now, focus on getting Scotland Yard where we want them."

"I will. Goodnight." Emmy smiles unconvincingly before leaving.

The morning of the funeral, Emmy is at Cliff's home by breakfast time. Lyn has brought her a cup of tea and now she is waiting for Cliff to join her. She isn't sure if she will be able to convince him, but she knows she has to try. For the dignity of Miss Davison, she has to try.

"Emmy, it is a surprise to see you here." Cliff enters the room, carrying his own cup of tea and a newspaper. Emmy wonders if it would have been so painful for him to add a "nice surprise" to the sentence.

"Yes, well, I have something important to discuss with you and I didn't want it to wait."

"Go ahead," he sits opposite her, trying to disguise the nervous twitch of his upper lip. As far as Cliff is concerned, Emmy must be here to either accept his proposal or refuse him for a second time. "I only have a few minutes before I must leave," he adds, in his most neutral tone of voice, which always comes out as cold and unfeeling.

"Of course, right. Well, it is about Emily Wilding Davison's funeral."

"That headache?" Cliff almost laughs as he says it. Not only was the entire situation with Miss Davison a complete nightmare for Cliff and his department at Scotland Yard, but that Emmy was here on business and not for the obvious personal issue that was hanging between them was cause for laughter. The impertinence of the girl was startling to Cliff, and yet, it drew him to her more and more.

"Yes, a headache, indeed." Emmy hides most of her sarcasm.

"What about it?"

"I have come to beg you to be lenient with the leaders of the WSPU today."

"What are you saying, Emmy? You are sounding like a sympathizer." Cliff puts his teacup down and stares hard into her eyes.

"I know it must seem that way. However, this is not in sympathy to the cause, but rather to human dignity and the right of Miss Davison to be laid to rest in the eyes of God without her friends being persecuted for trying to pay their respects."

"Why are you asking this?"

"I am asking this out of the moral obligation you have to protect the passing of a person, not a suffragette, but a person. If it were me instead, how would you want to grieve? How would you mourn me and lay me to rest if you knew you would be arrested as soon as you try to do the very basic thing we all need to do when someone we love passes on?" Emmy pleads.

"I will look weak if I do this," Cliff counters.

"You will look like a decent human being, Cliff. You will look respectful and kind, and as soon as the ordeal is over you can go back to what you do best, being ruthless. But please, for one day, try to be generous and allow these women the chance to mourn. They are deep in grief. Miss Davison was a dear friend to many within the WSPU, and they must be allowed to recognize her passing."

"Even though they have arranged a funeral procession throughout the streets of London that will cause madness and chaos?"

"Yes, even though they have done that. Show sympathy and you will come out on top, despite the grandiose nature of the funeral." Emmy lays her hand on his and Cliff looks down at the delicate fingers before letting out a loud sigh.

"Fine, if you insist. But I am doing this because you have asked me to, Emmy, and only because of that." Cliff marches towards the door. "Lyn will show you out."

An hour later at Cannon Row Station, Cliff calls a meeting of all his constables.

"Gather 'round, gather 'round!" Cliff yells out to the room and everyone crowds around him. He climbs on top of a chair so he can address everyone in the room.

"We are about to embark on a momentous day, gentlemen. The funeral procession of Emily Davison will march through our streets. We are anticipating thousands of women will be marching behind the casket and that thousands more will turn up to watch them go by. We have two duties today. First, our overall objective is to keep the peace. That means, unfortunate as it may be," Cliff smirks, "protecting the suffragettes that are in the procession."

The crowd of officers around him shout their objections and hiss under their breath.

"Gentlemen, gentlemen." Cliff motions for them to be quiet. "We will not have a repeat of Black Friday, understood? The Prime Minister and the King are expressly against anything like that occurring ever again."

The constables nod in understanding.

"Good, now on to the second objective. Mrs. Pankhurst will be attending this funeral. We have an outstanding arrest warrant for her under the Prisoners Temporary Discharge for Ill Health Act. You are instructed to arrest Mrs. Pankhurst, only after the funeral procession has reached its end point. We do not want to invoke a riot, we want to let the funeral come to the end and then arrest her while she is still in public view. Is that understood?"

"Yes, sir," the constables say in unison.

"Dismissed," Cliff commands with a smile.

"I still cannot believe that John gave you permission to come today," Emmy whispers to Edith. They are standing amongst thousands of women crowding into the street. It seems like every woman in London has come to be part of Miss Davison's funeral march, and more from outside London, too.

"I can't believe it either. To be honest, I don't think he had any idea that the funeral involved a public procession of suffragists. He likely thought I was just going to a peaceful church to pay my respects and would be home by tea time," Edith chuckles and a slight blush comes across her cheeks. Emmy has never known Edith to blush. She has always been an incredibly collected woman, even during her ordeal with Holloway and her husband refusing to allow her to return home to her children. Emmy looks at her friend with more scrutiny and watches as Edith works to regain composure.

"I can't lie to you," Edith adds to Emmy's questioning gaze. "It is lovely to be home again with the children, but John and I do not know how to act with each other. The tension is so high we are reduced to communicating through letters passed inside our own house."

"It's a start, I suppose," Emmy takes her friend's hand in her own and squeezes, not knowing what else to say.

Looking around her, Emmy sees women she recognizes from not just the Women's Social and Political Union, but also the Women's Tax Resistance League, the National Union of Women's Suffrage Societies, the Actresses' Franchise League, the Women Writers' Suffrage League, and even some members from the Men's League for Women's Suffrage. It is an unprecedented turnout and every single one of them is wearing white from head to toe.

Emmy and Edith are quite close to the front, along with Alice Sinclair. The crowd is getting anxious and Emmy feels the pressure of bodies pressing together in a tight space and wanting to move. Each small group talks quietly amongst themselves, but together, the noise is a loud rumbling sound that makes Emmy's heart race.

They need to get moving or else, Emmy fears, things will erupt. Looking ahead, Emmy can see the casket on its horse-drawn hearse, draped in purple, green, and white fabric and covered in flowers. Directly in front of them are the motor cars carrying Miss Sylvia Pankhurst and other WSPU leaders. Mrs. Pankhurst's empty motor sits proudly at the front of the motorcade, leading the way in vacant and silent tribute, while she stays hidden out of sight from the police. They had decided this was best, even though Emmy had Cliff's word that he would not arrest anyone. Mrs. Pankhurst was incredibly weak after her last stay in Holloway and was better off in bed and safely out of the way of Scotland Yard.

The procession finally begins and the horses set a pace that appeals to the large group of women walking behind them. As soon as they turn the corner and enter the main street, Emmy sees that on either side of their path, the road is lined with spectators, three rows deep, and there doesn't appear to be a gap at any point along the way. The crowd is eerily silent. Not like other WSPU marches Emmy has been in, where they shout and throw things towards the women. All that can be heard are the clicking of the horses' hooves, the slow hum of the motor cars, and the women's heels beating a steady rhythm.

Both on foot, and mounted on horseback, police constables are creating a human barrier between the procession and the spectators. Even they seem oddly silent.

Thoughts of the last time Edith and Emmy were in a march like this flood through Emmy's mind, causing her to breathe in short, panicked breaths.

"It is going to be fine, Emmy," Edith soothes, reading Emmy's mind. "This is a funeral, it isn't going to get violent like last time."

"How can you be sure?"

"Because people are more decent than that. Besides, you spoke to Cliff this morning, so we know the police are on our side."

"You are right, of course."

"I just wish Mrs. Pankhurst could have been here."

"Yes, she really should be sitting in that first motor car; it does seem odd without her. Although, I think it is making a statement."

"It is a powerful show, Alice was right about that," Edith adds, smiling towards their friend, who is deep in conversation with Annie Kenney, as they walk.

The procession goes on for some time. Someone began singing a few blocks back, breaking the terrible silence. The day is glorious with the sun beaming down on them and not a cloud in the sky. However, this made the ladies walking rather hot and tired, so they were all quite grateful when the procession takes an unexpected stop in front of Westminster Mansions.

"Finally." Edith dabs at the dainty beads of sweat that trickle down her forehead. "I am stifling."

"It is hot weather for a march," Emmy agrees, pulling at the stiff collar of the only white dress she could find to wear. "I wonder why we have stopped, though."

The mounted police struggle to keep their horses still with the ever-growing buzz from the crowds. Everyone is asking the same question as Emmy.

"Look," Edith points to the doors. "Someone is coming out."

Emmy looks up and, to her surprise, she sees Mrs. Pankhurst. Looking to Alice, she understands that this was secretly planned all along. Alice wears a smile that gives her away as the director of this melodrama. Emmy also sees, to her horror, the sudden movements of the mounted brigade and the constables on foot.

"What did you do?" Emmy says under her breath as she begins running towards Mrs. Pankhurst. She pushes past the ladies standing beside her who are still unaware of what is happening. Emmy isn't thinking about what she will do when she arrives. She can't very well go against the police without repercussions, but she also can't very well leave Mrs. Pankhurst up there alone thinking that the Yard has been taken care of and can be trusted to let her be. Emmy dodges the hooves of two big police horses and moves as fast as she possibly can through the crowd. Emmy can see very well how far Cliff's promise goes when the opportunity of arresting the great leader of the WSPU is presented.

Several other ladies are on the move towards Mrs. Pankhurst as well. Emmy doesn't see who they are, but she registers that they are all moving in the same direction at roughly the same speed. Emmy doesn't hear the cries of the people she shoves out of her way as she weaves through the throngs of onlookers and then slips past the police line back into the procession of suffragettes, trying to find the fastest route to Mrs. Pankhurst. One lady sails past them all and makes it to Mrs. Pankhurst before the rest of them. However, she is still too late. Emmy watches the scene as she runs, almost as if time is slowing down, allowing her to see all the details of the terrifying moment. Four constables surround Mrs. Pankhurst before she can even make it down the stairs. One of them grabs her arm and yanks it behind her back, twisting it as he goes. The poor, fragile woman's face distorts in pain as the four men roughly handle her sick body. She has barely recovered from the last hunger strike and has no muscle or fat left to soften the grips of the men. Then another detective manoeuvres her other arm behind her back and they begin carrying her away, just as Emmy's feet finally bring her to the bottom of the steps.

"Wait," she tries to call out after them, intending to show her badge and explain her deal with Cliff, but they are already gone into the crowd, and after running that fast, Emmy can hardly breathe, let alone yell.

Another woman runs up beside Emmy and in a blur of movement, Emmy thinks she sees her take down a constable but she isn't sure.

"I'm fine, thank you," Emmy hears someone say with a North American accent, and she looks up to see Gertrude Harding, the woman who executed the famed Orchid House attack. Standing beside her, and looking over the supine body of a constable, is a woman about as tall as Emmy's shoulder.

"That got a bit out of hand, I'd say," the woman spoke to Miss Harding.

"Forgive me," Emmy inserts herself into the conversation and moves up onto the steps and away from the jostling crowd. "Are you Gertrude Harding?"

"That's me," Miss Harding responds.

"I'm Emmy Nation. I was very impressed with your work in February. Quite the botanist," Emmy says to keep the true meaning of her praise a secret from listening ears.

"Thank you. I've heard of you as well, Miss Nation. You are very impressive yourself. Have you met Mrs. Garrud?"

"It's never been my pleasure," Emmy extends her hand. "Did you do this?" Emmy points to the constable who is slowly trying to get himself up.

"You should really pay closer attention to where you are going, officer." Mrs. Garrud offers her hand to him and winks at Emmy. "You took quite the tumble."

As the constable stands on his own two feet again and walks away, embarrassed by his "clumsiness", Emmy smiles at Mrs. Garrud, "I believe you must be *the* Edith Garrud, the jujitsu master, am I correct?"

"You are. And are you a practitioner yourself, or do you simply recognize the techniques?"

"I am a new practitioner—not near your level of experience or expertise."

"Well, you shall have to come by the dojo sometime and we can get you up to snuff." Edith Garrud nods her head curtly and walks away.

"Was that an invitation to train with her?" Emmy asks Miss Harding.

"I believe it was, Miss Nation, and one that you should consider a compliment."

"I will. It was lovely to finally meet you, Miss Harding."

"Likewise," Miss Harding smiles and returns to her place in the procession, which is beginning to move again.

Colin watches as Emmy rejoins Edith in the procession. He had been following her progress throughout the day and was certainly surprised to see her attempt to save Emmeline Pankhurst from arrest. She had no need to pretend to protect the leader of the WSPU. She was in a sea of women who could have stepped up and didn't. What was she playing at? He would have to be more vigilant and watch her more closely. Something was not right.

"How could you?" Emmy bursts into Cliff's office at Cannon Row Station. "You promised me."

"What are you talking about?" Cliff looks up from his papers, trying to hide the satisfaction he is feeling for arresting Mrs. Pankhurst.

"You promised you wouldn't arrest anyone, including Mrs. Pankhurst, at the funeral."

"Well, I can't be responsible for the entire Metropolitan Police Force, can I? I told the men from here not to arrest her. Were the arresting officers from this station?"

"I couldn't tell. But, still, you promised me, knowing that I was going to assure the ladies it was safe to mourn their friend, and you didn't uphold your promise."

"Forgive me, Emmy." Cliff softens as he stands up and closes the office door to the onlookers from outside. He gives them a stern, "back to work" face as he does. "I tried my best, but with so many officers in a city as large as London, and with so many stations represented when large public events like this happen, sometimes information does get lost in the shuffle." Cliff tries to assuage her anger with condescension in his voice. He takes her shoulders and guides her towards the chair. "Sit down, let me get you some tea. You look overwhelmed."

"I'm not overwhelmed, I'm mad, and don't try to calm me down. I can see through you; you think I am some dim-witted woman who you can control. Well, I put my position within the WSPU on the line today. I almost pulled out my badge—can you imagine where we would be now if I was kicked out of the suffrage leagues?"

"Emmy, Emmy." Cliff kneels in front of her and takes her delicate hand in his large palm. "I don't think you are a dim-witted woman. I love you. You know I love you. Please don't be mad at me. Come to dinner tonight and we can make up and be friends again. Please say you will come?"

Emmy looks at this grovelling man and wonders what he is about. Two years ago, she never could have imagined this behaviour from the cold, calculating Clifford

Marlowe. Is this all a ruse now, too, just as she was putting on, or had he truly changed into a man that expresses his feelings? Either way, he clearly still thought of her as a simpleton, that was always obvious in his tone of voice.

"I cannot," Emmy refuses.

"I see. You can't expect me to do your bidding, Emmy. I have a position here that requires certain actions. I will not sacrifice that for just any woman. If you were my wife, perhaps things would be different."

"I am not ready to give you an answer yet," Emmy tries to keep her composure as she says the words.

Cliff returns to his desk in silence. Sitting down, he looks back at Emmy.

"I do have things to attend to," he says, and turns to the papers he was working on when she arrived.

Emmy lets herself out of the office and returns to WSPU headquarters. She needs to find Sylvia Pankhurst, or General Drummond, even Annie Kenney, to explain what happened today.

CHAPTER 8

June 20, 1913

LYN STANDS ON THE street corner, her hat pulled low over her face, waiting until she sees Emmy return home from work. She knows Colin is not far behind, so she quickly catches up.

"Miss Nation," she calls softly behind Emmy.

"Lyn? I wasn't expecting to see you," Emmy turns and then pulls her inside after her. "Upstairs, quickly, before Colin arrives," Emmy instructs.

The pair race up to Emmy's flat and lock the door behind them.

"I have information for you, miss," Lyn explains.

"It was risky of you to come here like this. What if someone suspects you?"

"Don't worry so much. I am taking precautions. And, you've taught me well—I have a fake package for you that looks like the ones Mr. Marlowe is always sending you with dresses and jewellery and the like. But, I covered my tracks anyways."

"All right, go on, what news do you have?"

"The mole is not Mr. Thomas."

"Are you sure?" Emmy had not forgotten about the plan she had set with Miss Kerr to try to trap Colin, but with Miss Davison's funeral, their attention had been otherwise occupied and now she realizes how much time has passed since she first suspected him. "I can't think of anyone other than Colin who would know the information the mole had."

"The mole is a woman, that is all I know. I overheard Mr. Marlowe discussing it with someone on the telephone. He was most certainly speaking of his mole and he most certainly referred to her as a woman."

Emmy sits down, relief washing over her. She can trust Colin again and everything can go back to normal. Well, as close to normal as her life had ever been.

"I also overheard Mr. Marlowe say something about letting it slip to Mr. Thomas."

"What?" Emmy's interest sparked, and she looks at Lyn unsure. "What do you mean?"

"I am not sure, miss, but all I can think is that Mr. Marlowe wants Mr. Thomas to find out about the mole."

"I wonder why?" Emmy asks more to herself than to Lyn.

"I'm sure you will figure it out. I better be getting home, miss."

"Of course. Be safe." Emmy sees Lyn out the door.

An hour later, Colin slides a note under Emmy's door. On it he had written an address, a time, and the words "Meet me tonight." That was all.

At nine that evening, Emmy stands outside an old abandoned building. She double checks the address Colin had given her. She had the right place and was right on time, but there's no sign of life anywhere. She glances over her shoulder. It is a very dark and lonely street. Out of the corner of her eye, she thinks she sees a shadow and her body tenses. Her instincts kick in, making her ears pick up sounds she hasn't noticed before. The distant hoot of an owl, the wind rustling leaves on trees, but mainly she hears a few muffled footsteps. They sound heavy, like a man's. Then they come to an abrupt halt. The shadow had seen her turn. Emmy's mind races. She should rush inside and find Colin, if he is already inside. But if he isn't, she'll be trapped alone in a dark, creepy building. No, she determines, it would be better to stay on the street so she can run if she has to. The wind shifts, sending a gust towards

Emmy. A familiar smell comes with, it but she can't place it. The street light blows out with the wind, bringing even more darkness to the street.

"Bugger," Emmy says under her breath, feeling that her luck could not get any worse.

And then the shadow moves. It takes a step towards her and reaches out a hand. And then another step and another. Emmy is about to run when the shadow speaks.

"What's wrong," Colin's voice emerges from the dark silhouette. He starts looking around frantically, trying to find the source of the danger Emmy was feeling. "Were you followed?"

Emmy's heart skips a few beats before slowing back down to its normal pace.

"Yes, I was followed," she says. "By you, you bloody lout. Can you please tell me next time you will be following me late at night to an abandoned building where I am supposed to be meeting you? I assumed you would be waiting inside, not stalking me as usual."

"It's not stalking, it's my job. But, of course the next time we are meeting at an abandoned building late at night, I will let you know."

Emmy shivers, trying to shake off the tension in her body.

"I'm sorry I frightened you. I only meant to keep you safe," Colin says, instinctively placing his hand in Emmy's hand. For a moment, they linger in the touch, feeling the heat race through the contact.

Colin suddenly pulls back, abashed at his forwardness. He clears his throat and looks up at the building.

"The back window offers a perfect view into the alley. I have it on good authority that the mole for Scotland Yard makes a drop here. We will be able to track their movements from there."

"Ah, yes, perfect," Emmy says, also trying to recover the space that has always existed between them—the space that needed to exist between a man and a woman. "What is a drop?"

"It is when you leave something for another person to pick up. For example, I might write you a note on a newspaper and then drop the newspaper in a waste bin for you to come by afterwards and pick up. Then we are never in the same place together."

"Oh, I see. Sounds very sneaky and like quite a dirty task."

Inside the building, Emmy climbs the dark stairs first. She feels Colin's eyes avoiding her. She has become accustomed to him watching her from a distance, but tonight it feels different, and when she sneaks a look back at him, his eyes are steadfastly staring at the floor. They had touched many times before, but this touch felt more intimate, like they had let their guards down for that moment. Emmy liked it. She wanted to let her guard down again, but Colin had put his back up quickly and he was putting forth an impenetrable front.

They reach their destination and Colin leads the way into a deserted room.

"We have to keep the lights off so no one can see us from the street," Colin says, while looking towards the window and not at Emmy.

The street lamps illuminate the alley they need to watch, and some of the light spills into the room with a flickering soft glow, giving it a romantic air. Or perhaps Emmy just feels that way because of their earlier trespass. Either way, Emmy knew what Mrs. Lawrence would say if she could see her now. *"A wildly inappropriate situation for a nice young man like Mr. Thomas to put a nice young woman like you in."*

"So now we just wait?" Emmy asks, as Colin carries two dusty, hard chairs over to the windows.

"Now we just watch," Colin corrects her. He sits and looks out the window. Silence.

"I'm really good at watching. Just watch me," Emmy jokes, trying to lift Colin's mood. It doesn't work. So, they sit in silence, looking out the window, hoping for something to happen soon.

"You do not have to stay, this is WSPU business, not Scotland Yard's," Emmy breaks the silence.

"Emmy, I want to know who the mole is as much as you. Marlowe is getting inside information that is counteracting the information you are passing on. That does not make either of us look good. I want to get to the bottom of this for my job, just as much for yours. Besides, I am not leaving you out here all alone. Who knows who this snitch is. You might need backup."

"Considering that it is most likely a woman from the WSPU, I hardly think I will need backup. Plus, I have received the best jujitsu training in all of London. My teacher is really top-notch." Emmy smiles.

"Oh, stop trying to suck up, Miss Nation. Your powers of persuasion are lost on me," Colin jokes. The truth was anything but.

Around ten that evening, almost a full hour of awkward silence later, they finally see movement in the street. Colin sits up. Emmy jumps to her feet and steps towards the window.

"Not so close, Emmy," Colin whispers as he grabs her hand to pull her back. Emmy feels her arm absorb the warmth of his touch for the second time that evening, and it spreads through her whole body while setting off shivers in the pit of her stomach. Colin doesn't seem to notice his hand on hers this time. He is focused outside.

A man is standing by the door to the building across the street and not leaving. Instead, he pulls out a hand-rolled cigarette and lights it. Then he pulls out a flask from his pocket and drinks.

"It must be the janitor from that building taking a break," Colin says, while looking at his watch. "At two minutes past ten. Remember that, Emmy, just in case he is the mole," he adds before finally looking up at her. His hand is still clasped around hers, but it softens as their eyes meet. Emmy squeezes Colin's hand hard and doesn't let go. She never wants to let go.

"You should stand farther back from the window," Colin explains. "The sudden movement might catch his eye and give us away." Colin pulls her farther back into the room, and their eyes stay locked on each other until they are far enough away from the window that they cannot be seen. With his other hand, Colin reaches out and runs his fingers up Emmy's arm. The wind blows outside, knocking branches together and rustling the leaves, but there is no sound inside.

Emmy takes a step closer. She wants to be in his arms. Colin's hand reaches her shoulder and then her cheek.

Emmy notices that it is trembling and she takes it in her hand to steady it.

"Emmy," Colin begins, but doesn't finish. So, she steps closer once again, reaches up slightly and kisses him on the lips, finishing his thought for him. It is a short, sweet kiss. One you might give your mother, but it was a kiss.

"Emmy, we shouldn't..."

"I know," she replies but barely gets the words out before Colin crushes her into his arms and kisses her with every ounce of passion that has been building up since he first laid eyes on her at the Cannon Row Police Station. Emmy's heart pounds and she feels Colin's beating in tune with hers through his chest. She wants to stay in this moment forever, never returning to the day-to-day moments of regular life.

Emmy had only kissed one man before, Clifford Marlowe. The first time, they had discussed kissing beforehand and had both agreed that they should try it once before they were married. So, they stood up from the bench in the garden, turned to face each other, adjusted because the sun was in Cliff's eyes, leaned in, and put their lips together. It was technical and emotionless. Their second kiss had been much worse.

Colin's kiss, on the other hand, is everything a kiss should be, and Emmy melts into him, hoping it might last forever. But all good kisses must come to an end and theirs ended with the slam of a door from below.

The pair separates as fast as they can disentangle themselves.

"What was that?" Emmy whispers. Colin creeps to the window.

"The janitor. He went back inside. Break time is over. It is six minutes past ten, remember that," he says, looking from his watch up to her and then diverting his eyes as fast as he can.

Long kiss, Emmy thinks, before taking her seat again.

"Wait, someone is coming," Colin points to the end of the street, towards a dark shadow approaching. It is a man's figure that walks slowly and aimlessly. He stops under the street lamp, giving Emmy and Colin a perfect view of his face.

"That's Officer Black," Colin states, surprised.

"Look, from the other direction." Emmy points. "A woman is coming." The pair watch as a well-dressed lady approaches Officer Black. She holds in her hand an envelope. They can't make out much more than that until she reaches the street lamp.

Emmy's jaw drops. It can't be. This couldn't be true; it couldn't be happening. On the street below, clearly meeting with Clifford Marlowe's informant was her dear friend, Edith.

Emmy grabs her hat and races towards the door.

"Emmy, you can't go down there," Colin reaches the door first, blocking her path.

"I have to. Edith needs me, she is obviously in trouble, otherwise she wouldn't be doing this." Emmy pushes him out of the way and Colin does not struggle against her. Instead he rushes back to the window to watch. Thankfully, Officer Black is already turning to leave. Edith returns the same way she came down the street.

Just as Officer Black is rounding the corner, Emmy emerges from the building. She rushes out into the street towards Edith. She can't believe what she has just seen. It can't be true. Not Edith, not her Edith. She runs down the street towards her friend as fast as she can.

"Edith!" Emmy calls to her, the anger and hurt rising to the surface through her voice. Edith stops and turns around, and her body freezes at the sight of Emmy getting closer.

"Emmy, what are you doing here?" Edith asks, eyes filling with tears as she sees in her friend's eyes that her secret has been revealed.

"I was trying to find out who the mole is."

"Oh." Edith doesn't know what to say.

"Edith, tell me it's not true. Tell me you are here doing the same thing," Emmy searches her friend's face for a sign that she is innocent, but sees only shame.

"I can't."

"Edith, why? How? How could you do this?"

"You're one to lecture, Miss Undercover Suffragette," Edith stabs the words without really meaning to. She had forgiven Emmy for her betrayal, but now that the tables are turned, she is having a hard time forgiving herself.

"I guess I deserve that, but what I did was wrong, so very wrong, and you helped me to see that. You changed me, made me into a better person and a true believer in the cause and the WSPU. Edith, it was all you. You made me into a double agent. I am here only because of you. How could you be working for the enemy? You are the most ardent believer."

"I have my reasons," Edith closes off, not sure if Emmy will understand.

"Tell me, I deserve at least that."

"You don't. You don't know anything. It is all your fault that John took me away from my children. You pushed me into more militant actions and it was you that wanted to do the Portrait Gallery job. I was just supporting you, my friend, and look where that got me. In jail, tortured, on the edge of death, and without my children."

"But John forgave you; you are back with your children now."

"No, John hasn't forgiven me anything. I am practically under house arrest living in that home. I am willing to live that way because I am with my children again, but it is not a real life."

"Why did he let you back then?" Emmy asks, although she feels the answer already.

"Why do you think? I was given a choice. Scotland Yard is desperate for any spies they can get, not just you, their golden girl. They want more. So, John made a deal. If they let me out of prison, I would spy on the WSPU for them. That's how he got me out. And, then he held my children ransom. If I ever wanted to see them again, I would have to become an undercover suffragette, just like my dear friend, Emmy." Edith's words hit Emmy like a ton of bricks. She stumbles backwards, feeling her legs turn to mush beneath her. She reaches out and grabs onto the stone wall of the building behind her for support. Her heart sinks. What had she done?

"Oh, Edith," she finally says. "Oh, Edith, I am so sorry. I have messed everything up. You must hate me. I am so sorry. You are my closest friend and I have ruined your life." The tears pour down Emmy's cheeks, leaving wet streaks of shame for her to wear as penance for her betrayals.

"Emmy," Edith's voice is softer now and she places a gentle hand on Emmy's arm. "Emmy, I have to do this, for my children. I am sorry." She walks down the street, disappearing around the corner, leaving Emmy alone and ashamed.

Colin waits until Edith has left before leaving the building. He takes Emmy by the waist and holds her tight against his warm body. "Let's go home," he says, while he wipes tears off her face. "Let's go home and have a warm cuppa."

"What do I do now?"

"Sshh, it will be all right, Emmy. It will be all right."

"Do I tell? Do I tell Mrs. Pankhurst about this? I've already gotten Edith into so much trouble already."

"You will figure it out tomorrow. Right now, let's go home."

CHAPTER 9

June 23-July 11, 1913

EMMY LOOKS OUT THE window near her desk. The sky has just turned the shade of dark grey that comes out of the smokestacks from the factories down by the Thames. It was bound to burst open in a downpour at any moment. The wet winter months had turned into wet summer months, but at least Emmy doesn't have to wear boots with holes in them anymore.

Her work sits half-finished on the desk in front of her. One page sticks up out of the typewriter, a sentence still hanging in the air waiting for completion. The dark sky makes Emmy want to close her eyes, to sleep. Just a little nap. It didn't have to be long. Ten minutes, or twenty minutes. What she would give for a full hour of sleep. Imagine that. Sixty minutes in her bed at home, rain tapping softly against the window, covers pulled up high, keeping all the heat in and the cold out. Glorious, wonderful, heavenly—

"Bugger," her tea spills onto her lap, burning her skin through layers of skirts.

She is fully awake now, despite her exhaustion. She turns back to her typewriter, putting her teacup safely down on her desk. The paragraph she was in the middle of transcribing made no sense at all. Words were missing or misspelled, she had repeated one sentence four times in a row, and she had missed an entire section of the original editorial. She absolutely needed more sleep. Even a vacation?

Could she take a vacation? The idea swirls around inside her. Is it possible? Who would she ask? Cliff? Colin? Mrs. Pankhurst? And where would she go?

In a daze, Emmy stands up and goes to the kettle in the little kitchenette the ladies had set up in one corner of the offices. She fills her teacup without realizing she is doing so and returns to her desk. She could go to Mae's. Mae had plenty of space for houseguests, unlike the Rose Garden Cottage. And, Mae had taken on Emmy's childhood horse when Emmy sold Nation Manor, so she could go riding. Of course, she wouldn't mind being near her mother either, or meeting Mae's new baby.

Emmy looks out the window again to where the rain had started to come down in a heavy sheet. She will write to Mae this evening and ask if she can visit for a few days.

Then she will have to ask Cliff and Mrs. Pankhurst, but she would make it very clear that she could not go on without a vacation. She hadn't slept since she had discovered Edith's secret. She still hadn't decided what to do about it, and Colin had not said anything about that night either. Did he suspect her of being loyal to the WSPU? It had all been swirling around her mind, giving her no chance of rest. Yes, she needs to get out of London to sleep and think.

It was easier than she thought it would be to convince Cliff and Mrs. Pankhurst to let her take some time off, and a few days later, Emmy is sitting in the window of Mae's library, enjoying a view of the gardens. A book lay open, but unread, in her lap. She hadn't been able to concentrate on her book since she arrived. Her mind was too full, too tired. She kept turning both events over and over in her mind. Reliving the wonderful moment with Colin and then the devastating blow from Edith. Edith had been right though, Emmy had driven her to this action. It was all Emmy's fault that Edith's life had been turned upside down. She must inform Mrs. Pankhurst. Although she loves Edith and understands why she was spying, Emmy had devoted herself to the WSPU and she must help the women at all costs. Maybe Edith will even be relieved to not have to spy on her friends anymore. If she is discovered by the WSPU, she will be of no use to the police anymore and she can go back to a peaceful life with her children.

"Emmy," Mae broke her thoughts. "Your mother is just arriving."

"Thank you," Emmy looks up. Mae is holding her new baby, wrapped in a sky-blue blanket.

"He is beautiful, Mae. Truly, and so are you." Emmy kisses her friend on the cheek.

"We are happy you are here with us, aren't we baby boy?" Mae coos down at her little bundle, his tiny face barely visible amongst the folds of blanket.

"I shall go meet her on the path," Emmy announces to Mae.

"Would you like tea brought in for you?" Mae asks.

"Yes, please," Emmy says, as she brushes her finger against the soft cheek of baby Gregory. "We won't be long."

Emmy gets the report from her mother on the walk up to the house. All the suffragettes who are staying with her are on the mend. Most are nearly healthy enough to face the question of what to do next. Go back home to London and risk rearrest, or move on to more permanent country living in secret?

"It is quite a nice place right now, my dear," her mother adds. "Without anyone really sick anymore, we are having quite a bit of fun. The ladies enjoy spending time in the garden or taking Charlie for long walks. And we almost always stay up late playing cards. I have never had companionship like this before."

"And the WSPU is ever so grateful to you."

It isn't until they are inside that Emmy tells her mother and Mae about Edith. She leaves out Colin for the time being. They take it rather well, both with a pat on her shoulder and sympathetic ear. And then they pass the evening in greater joy until it is time to retire to bed. Emmy finally sleeps, peacefully and deeply.

But, she wakes up in the morning to a scream from her mother.

"What's wrong," Emmy races into the room her mother had slept in.

"It's the cottage," Mrs. Nation points out her window. Emmy looks out to see a devastating scene. The cottage is surrounded by police and, one by one, the suffragettes who were hidden inside to recover are marched out to a waiting truck.

"And here I am in my nightdress, with a tray of breakfast waiting for me. I should be there with them," Mrs. Nation begins to put on her jacket and boots.

"No, Mother, you cannot go down there. By some miracle, you are here and not there—you have been saved."

"I cannot abandon my friends in their time of need. I am the captain, I must go down with the ship."

"And then what? You will all be in jail together and we will have no ship to sail at all."

"Emmy," her mother looks as stern as she did when Emmy was a child and had gotten into something she was not supposed to.

"Mother," Emmy returns the gaze. "I will not let you sacrifice yourself. I have been to jail. I know what they do. I will not let you if I have to hold you down myself until they are gone."

"How did they know, Emmy?"

"I swear I never told Edith about the Rose Garden Cottage. She must have known that you were going to move—she knew that I was selling Nation Manor. But, I promise, I never told her where you were going. I never told her that the sale was complete. Although I suppose she would have known that after they raided the house," Emmy runs through her memories trying to find a time she might have let the news slip to Edith. But, no, she had kept it secret. She was sure. She hadn't even told Colin where she was moving her mother.

Mrs. Nation sits on the edge of the bed, tears running down her face.

"Are they still there?" she finally asks.

Emmy looks out the window again. "No, they are just driving away."

From the window, Emmy sees Charlie chase the trucks down the laneway, barking at the men who had taken away his friends. But, he doesn't leave the cottage property. Instead he returns to the front door, lies downs, and waits for Mrs. Nation to return.

Emmy continues to run through her memories. Had she told Edith about the Rose Garden Cottage? She cannot remember, but now her mind is made up. She must write to Mrs. Pankhurst at once and tell her about Edith's betrayal. She must try to prevent any other breach of information that might put one of her sister suffragettes in this same position. As much as she did not want to send her friend to the gallows, Emmy had made her choice on that night not long ago when she became a double agent. She had chosen freedom or death, the cause over everything else, including her closest friends.

CHAPTER 10

July 16-17, 1913

EMMY HAD WRITTEN TO Cliff to schedule a dinner the same day the Rose Garden Cottage had been raided. She had put off answering his marriage proposal for too long. After the discovery that Edith was the mole and then the raid on all those poor women, Emmy was determined to do the right thing. She was not going to betray Colin. They had kissed—it was confirmed that their feelings were mutual and she was not going to give that up to further the cause. Mrs. Pankhurst would understand. As Edith had said about her own situation, some lives are not really lives at all, and Emmy did not want to be a prisoner inside Cliff's house. Even if she didn't have the ear of and the inside scoop at Scotland Yard, she would be far more useful to the WSPU if she were free to do what she wanted.

She wears her own dress to dinner, not one that Cliff had given her. It is simpler than all his fashion choices, but still elegant. She feels confident in it—powerful—and that is what she needs this evening.

The butler opens the door for her, but Emmy sees Lyn standing in the doorway leading down to the kitchen. Lyn can sense that something has changed in Emmy. She doesn't say anything, but gives her a smile that makes Emmy feel safe and protected. No matter what was about to happen, Emmy had an ally inside Cliff's house.

"Emmy, you look lovely," Cliff greets her with hesitation in his voice, looking her up and down, clearly not approving of the dress choice. "Come to the drawing room. Are we close to dinner?"

"Yes, sir. Very close," the butler responds with a nod and leaves the room.

"Well, Emmy," Cliff begins, not really sure where to end, for once in his life. They hadn't been alone together since the fight and he isn't sure how to act around her. He wants to just demand an answer, but he knows better than to pressure her. That had not worked out in his favour last time around. "Can I offer you a refreshment?" he finally asks.

"No, I'm fine, thank you. Actually, I don't believe I will be staying for dinner, Cliff," Emmy says, gathering her courage. "I just came to answer your question, your marriage proposal."

"And you aren't staying for dinner, meaning your answer is no." Cliff's face flushes with anger and embarrassment.

"My answer is no. I am deeply sorry, Cliff. I really did put a lot of thought into this decision. I have enjoyed our dinners together and getting to know you more intimately. You are not the person I thought you were two years ago, you are much more than that, and someone who I could have seen myself married to if it weren't for—" Emmy stops herself.

"If it weren't for Colin," Cliff finishes her sentence. He moves to the decanter sitting on the mantel, hiding his face from Emmy. He pours a tumbler of whiskey in silence, waiting for Emmy to confirm or deny.

"If it weren't for my desire to remain independent. I've been living on my own for over two years now, and I cannot describe to you the freedom and joy that brings me. I feel like a person, not just a woman, but a person, who answers to no one but herself. Can you understand that, Cliff? Do you remember what it felt like when you finally emerged from under your father's shadow and became a man of your own, with your own home and business and status in society? Do you remember that feeling? That is what living on my own is for me. I am not ready to give that up for you or for Colin."

"So, you are a suffragette," Cliff swallows his whiskey in one mouthful and grits his teeth together.

"I am loyal to Scotland Yard, but I am not the girl you met two years ago. I am a new woman. An independent woman. I cannot go back. Please understand that, Cliff."

"Do not deny it, Miss Nation," Cliff's tone changes. It is no longer just anger, but a darkness seeps in at the corners of it. "I know about the Rose Garden Cottage."

"Yes, I was at Mae and Robert's house for the week," Emmy tries to cover the anxiety rising from her stomach. "It was raided while I was there by the local police on a tip from Scotland Yard. I believe they found some suffragettes hiding there as they recovered from their hunger striking." Emmy manages to keep her voice calm, although she is glad that Cliff is still not looking at her.

"Stop lying to me, I have seen the deed for the cottage," Cliff turns to face her, his face the colour of a tomato ripe for eating. "You purchased it after your father's house sold, and your mother is the one running this hospice for suffragettes. I have the proof, Emmy, so stop with your falsehoods," he crosses to her and finishes with his face only inches from hers. Emmy does not know how to respond. She has been found out. If he has the deed of the house, he has the evidence to condemn her for aiding and abetting the fugitive suffragettes. And there is no way to save her mother from implication either. Of course, Mrs. Nation would be the lady of the house in Emmy's name. She had nowhere else to live.

"Cat got your tongue, little mouse?" Cliff's whiskey breath pours over Emmy, making her stomach wrench. Emmy suppresses the urge to vomit before speaking again.

"Cliff, if you know, then what do you want from me?" Emmy finally says, holding her ground.

"I want you to marry me," he answers simply.

"Why would you possibly want to marry me? I have clearly betrayed you, betrayed Scotland Yard, and am quite obviously working with your very enemy, the WSPU."

"You still don't get it, do you? I am in love with you, despite my better judgement, and I will have you." Cliff finally stands up and moves away from her, retreating to the whiskey and another mouthful.

"If you love me, you will let me do what I want," Emmy counters.

"If I love you, I will have you," Cliff demands.

"No, you won't." It is a simple statement, but it fills the room with heaviness.

"Then I'll have your mother arrested. She won't be afforded any luxuries in Holloway. I will make sure she is force fed, even if she does not hunger strike," Cliff counters, grasping at the first thing he can use as leverage.

"You will have to find her first," Emmy keeps her voice steady. She had left Mae with the task of keeping Mrs. Nation hidden and safe, but she will have to move her to a new location soon. In fact, she will have to do better than just hide her. The look on Cliff's face tells Emmy that he will stop at nothing. Emmy has to make her disappear. She will not let her mother be tortured because of her unwillingness to marry this monster. She must protect her at all costs.

Cliff does not respond and does not turn around to face her, instead he throws his glass at the wall. It hits with a crash that rings through the silent room, then the glass, smattered in tiny fragments, pings as it hits the floor. Emmy quietly leaves the drawing room. Lyn is waiting outside for her. The fear on her face fades into that smile again when she sees that Emmy is ok. She quickly squeezes Emmy's hand.

"Thank you for your friendship, Lyn," Emmy squeezes back.

"It is still yours, Miss Emmy. The motor car is waiting to take you home."

"Thank you." Emmy smiles and leaves Cliff's house for the last time.

"Wait," Emmy says to the chauffeur. "Turn here instead." She points down the street. She isn't ready to go home and see Colin yet. She isn't sure what all this means. Instead, she directs the car to a different house, not far from where Cliff lives. It is grand from the outside and when she is shown into the drawing room to wait, she sees that it is equally grand on the inside as well.

"Emmy, is that you?" Gwen twitters, sashaying into the library in a gorgeous gown of light blue organza.

"Sorry to just arrive uninvited."

"Nonsense. Please sit down." Gwen points to a chair and then turns back to a footman in the corner. "Would you bring us some tea, please, Henry?"

"I didn't know where else to go or who else to talk to," Emmy breaks down as soon at the footman is out the door. "I'm sorry to blubber like this, it's just that everything seems to be falling down around me."

"Now, it can't be that bad. Why don't you tell me all about it?" Gwen hands Emmy a handkerchief and takes her hand in her own.

"Well, you were there through it all, really. From my first day on the job, that day Mr. Johnson asked you to go undercover but he got me instead. Sometimes I wish you had said yes and I had gone on living the way I was, with Mrs. Lawrence and leaking boots."

"Emmy, darling, you were meant for your job, while I was meant for this one. Go on, tell me what happened."

"Cliff asked me to marry him, again, as you know. And Colin kissed me, which you don't know. And Edith is working as a mole for Scotland Yard, all because of me and the betrayal of our friendship. I ruined her life completely and now I fear that I am ruining my mother's and Colin's at the same time."

"And what of your life?"

"What of it? I feel as though I am barely keeping my head above water. At any point my limbs could fail me and I will just sink to the bottom, lost forever to the mad chaos of this city."

"You really need this tea," Gwen motions for Henry to bring in the tea service. "Thank you," she dismisses him, leaving the two of them in private again. Gwen pours two cups and Emmy is grateful for the familiar warmth.

"Now, tell me everything," Gwen insists.

Emmy tells her all the gritty details of the events that had happened with the WSPU and the Met, Edith, her mother, Colin, and now Cliff. At the end of the story, she feels a sense of relief at sharing it all with someone outside of the drama.

"Well, you've really got yourself mixed up, darling."

"I don't know what to do. How can I go home? How can I go back to the WSPU?"

"First off, don't worry about Cliff now. You've ended that relationship and you will find a way to protect your mother from him. It seems to me that Colin is holding you back from doing what you really want to do."

"What is that?" Emmy asks, surprised.

"Committing fully to the WSPU." Gwen states this so simply, it seems as though she is suggesting Emmy just put a hat on her head and she will be done.

"I don't know if I can. That would mean leaving Scotland Yard and putting Colin in a very uncomfortable position."

"Yes, it would," Gwen adds. "I believe that after this evening your career at Scotland Yard is over and besides, you have to do what is in your heart, Emmy."

"You surprise me, you know?"

"How so?"

"You are always so upbeat and focused on superficial things that I sometimes forget how deeply intelligent and insightful you are."

"I play the part that was given to me to play. You know this—you do the same thing."

"I suppose we all do to some extent."

"And I suppose that is what we are all fighting for, each in our own way. Edith, too."

"I know. I don't blame her. I joined the enemy simply for the promise of new boots."

"Emmy Nation, you have been incredibly brave. If anyone can overcome this, it is you." Gwen kisses her on the cheek and sees her out into the warm night breeze.

Emmy knocks three times and then pauses for a beat before her last rap on the door to Mrs. Pankhurst's secret office.

"Come in," the voice rings out from the other side, and Emmy opens the door to see the leaders of the WSPU all huddled around a map on the large desk in the centre of the office. The morning sun pours in through the open window and fills the room with warmth. Mrs. Pankhurst and Annie Kenney look frail next to the stocky form of General Drummond, even though the General has endured her fair share of hunger striking and force feeding in Holloway.

"Sorry I'm late," Emmy apologizes. "I had a heck of a time getting away from Colin this morning. I think with the Edith thing, he has become increasingly worried about my safety." She decides to leave out the altercation with Cliff and her assumed firing from Scotland Yard. Not before she knows why they have called her to this early morning meeting and what they want from her.

"Not to worry, dear," Mrs. Pankhurst assures, "we were just getting started."

"Yes, sit, Emmy," Mrs. Drummond commands, and Emmy sits.

"We have an assignment for you and you will likely need to gather some other ladies to assist you in it." Mrs. Pankhurst sits behind the desk and pulls out a piece of paper.

"What is it?"

"Mrs. Williams is due to leave on her tour of Canada on Thursday."

"Yes, I remember. I was at her house for her practice speech and yours as well. The Freedom or Death speech."

"So, you know how important it is that we both make it to our tours. We need to spread our message in North American to help our sisters achieve their own freedom. Besides, if we stay in England, we will be giving in to the demands of the government. We need to show them that they cannot control us, that we will continue to fight even when they try to silence us."

"Of course, but how can I help?"

"Well, Mrs. Williams has gotten herself in a little situation."

"It is a large situation, if you ask me," Mrs. Drummond adds.

"Oh, Flora, it is not that bad. We've dealt with worse," Annie chimes in.

"Sure, we've dealt with worse, but you would think Mrs. Williams would have had the good sense to keep her nose out of it this close to her departure date."

"Nevertheless, we are in this situation, and it is imperative that Mrs. Williams gets on the boat to Canada," Mrs. Pankhurst interrupts.

"What has happened?" Emmy inquires before another squabble can occur.

"Mrs. Williams took part in a rather public display of militancy the other day and has been in Holloway ever since."

"I cannot break her out of Holloway, Mrs. Pankhurst. That is beyond my capabilities."

"You won't need to. Her husband has bailed her out, so she should be home tomorrow. The trouble is, Scotland Yard seems intent on keeping her in prison. The judge has agreed to release her on bail, but he has added several conditions to her release. First and foremost is that she will not leave the city. Not to mention that she will not participate in any suffrage activities, privately or publicly, for the next ninety days, including travelling for any suffrage engagements. She must also be chaperoned wherever she goes by one of her staff, who is under the most ardent orders to report back to the police should Mrs. Williams do anything related to the suffrage movement."

"Well, that is a bugger of a situation," Emmy sighs.

"We need your help, Emmy." Annie places a hand over Emmy's. "We need your skills and your knowledge of the Met."

"We need you to make sure Mrs. Williams gets on her boat. We have our sisters from the Southampton chapter planning her trip from the train to the pier, but we need to get her out of her house and to the train station in London. Can you help us?" Mrs. Drummond asks.

"Yes, I think I can. But it won't be easy. I've just come under quite a bit of scrutiny at Scotland Yard and, like I said, Colin has become even more protective of me and is hardly letting me out of his sight. I will need to plan this well and, as you suggested, get a team of ladies to help me execute it," Emmy lies, but an opportunity presented itself and she is determined to take it.

"It is imperative that you do not get found out, Emmy. You are too important to the cause to be arrested now.

You must protect yourself at all costs," Mrs. Pankhurst adds.

"But Mrs. Williams is more important," Mrs. Drummond begins.

"No, Flora, Emmy is more important in this case. If Mrs. Williams does not make it to Canada that is the problem of the Canadians. Fine people, but they do have to fight their own fight after all. Emmy is our link to the world of the police and to the politicians. She is not only entrenched in Scotland Yard, but also with Clifford Marlowe. We cannot afford to lose both of those advantages. Mrs. Williams can postpone her visit, but we cannot postpone Emmy's insider information. However, for the political statement, it is much preferred that Mrs. Williams gets on that boat."

Emmy is about to speak up about her falling-out with Cliff, but she decides against it for now. This is a very big task they are giving her, and she believes she can do it, with or without her hold over Cliff. She still has Lyn, and she still knows more about Cliff than anyone else. She can deceive him even if she isn't his fiancée.

"I suppose you are right. Emmy, you let me know what you need. I will do all I can to help you."

"Thank you, Mrs. Drummond. I will come up with a plan of attack and get back to you. I think it best, however, if we keep as much of the plan to ourselves as possible. I fear it will be some time before I fully trust anyone again."

"Emmy, we were all fooled by Edith, as we were with you before you revealed yourself to us. In both cases, your actions came from a place of goodness, and we cannot forget that. Edith is still in our hearts as a sister of suffrage. She did what she had to do to be with her children, as any mother would," Annie soothes.

"You are right, of course, Miss Kenney. I try to remind myself of that every day, but still it hurts. I did the same to her though, and she forgave me. Edith was my closest friend and I must remember that and not dwell on the other. Regardless, I shall be needing our most loyal and trustworthy fighters for this mission. Mrs. Drummond, perhaps you can suggest a few women you trust?"

"Absolutely. I will send you the best."

"Emmy," Mrs. Pankhurst adds, "you are right, the fewer of us who know the details, the better. Those of us in this room do not need to be privy to your plan. Neither does Mrs. Williams. Keep it as small and contained as possible. Only those who are involved in the execution of the plan need know the details. The fewer people who can leak the information, the safer we will all be. I fear that many in our ranks have been shaken by recent events, and we will discover more moles and turncoats amongst ourselves soon."

"I understand, Mrs. Pankhurst. I will keep the details close. Now, when did you say Mrs. Williams leaves for Canada?"

"In two days."

"Two days! That does not leave much time at all."

"No, Emmy, you must work quickly on this one."

"All right. Mrs. Drummond, send me those women tonight. We will meet in the usual place. I will have something thought up by then. Now, I have a request for you." Emmy sits back in her chair trying to appear at ease.

"Go on," Mrs. Pankhurst looks wary.

"My mother has been nursing women back to health, and her home has been raided, as you know. I believe it may not be long before she and I are found out to be the owners of the cottage. She is currently being protected by a friend, but she can't stay hidden forever. I want her to go to Canada with Mrs. Williams. She has a cousin there she could stay with, and she will be quite safe from the Met on the other side of the Atlantic."

Mrs. Pankhurst sits silently for some time before she speaks.

"It is a reasonable request, Miss Nation, and as you are the one planning this escape to Canada, I will allow you to include your mother in the events. Flora will connect the Southampton ladies with all the details they need."

"Thank you." Emmy smiles.

"Good luck, my dear," Mrs. Pankhurst adds as Emmy reaches the door.

"I will do my best," Emmy nods before she leaves. "And do my best quickly," she adds to the empty hallway. Emmy starts out for home, desperate to put her feet up and forget the problems of the world for one night. But if she can get her mother out of Cliff's warpath, she will have a much easier time relaxing. She needs to figure out the details for her mother first, then send a telegram to relay them. She will have to risk it being intercepted; she simply did not have time for anything else. The rest of the plan can come later.

CHAPTER 11

July 17, 1913

EMMY SPENDS THE AFTERNOON in her flat alone. That is to say, she tries to spend the afternoon in her flat alone. Colin is home for the day as well, and keeps coming up with excuses to knock on her door and check up on her. Finally, she gives him the definitive signal to leave her alone—she claims to have a headache and says she needs to stay in bed, alone, with the lights low for the rest of the day.

Now, with a cup of tea in front of her, a map of London, and her notepad, she works. The plan must account for various things and many different scenarios. First and foremost, the boat is due to leave in the afternoon, and Emmy does not want Mrs. Williams to arrive too early. The closer to departure time she gets on the boat, the less time the police will have to find her. But, this will mean that all of London will be awake and bustling, especially at the train station. Emmy is determined to make this into a positive. Crowds of people mean that they can easily blend in, unlike leaving under cover of night, as they had done with Marion Campbell, when they were some of the only people on the street. However, crowds also mean more police officers and more bodies in the way, on top of the fact that people are always unpredictable. Emmy simply could not rely on anything to go as planned if it were happening in the middle of a group of strangers, who may or may not be friendly to the cause.

The best idea Emmy has come up with is more complicated than she would like, and involves more people than she can ever hope to trust completely. But with little time to come up with something new, she must pray that it will all work out. She will need to gather the troops that she can rely on, along with several items that they will need to execute the deception.

Emmy writes out a list of what they will need to pull this off.

1. *Disguises—really good disguises. (Enlist Alice Sinclair immediately.)*

2. *A false reason for Mrs. Williams to host a small gathering of women in her house. (To be determined.)*

3. *Invitations to this fake gathering.*

4. A ticket for a different passenger to get on the boat to Canada and a reason for her to go. (Mrs. Drummond to connect with Southampton chapter.)

5. False documentation for Mrs. Williams. (Mrs. Drummond to secure.)

Emmy is going to need some help if she is going to get this all done before the meeting that evening.

She knocks quietly on Colin's door so as not to alarm him.

"Colin?" she says softly into the keyhole.

"I'm here, I'm coming," he calls back and opens the door into his own flat. "How are you feeling?"

"A bit better, but I could use some more mint leaves to help with my headache."

"I will go get you some. Don't worry, Emmy, I will be right back."

"Bless you, Colin," she adds to heighten the effect. She waits at her window to see him exit the building and turn the corner before she also leaves. Throwing on her coat, she runs downstairs and heads towards the post office on the corner.

"Hello there, Miss Nation," the officer behind the desk greets her. "What can I do for you today?"

"Hello, Mr. Jackson. I just need to make a quick telephone call."

"Of course, go right ahead. You can pay after you are done."

"Thank you. I will need privacy though. You do understand, don't you?"

"Absolutely, yes. You know how to use one of these machines?"

"We have them at Cannon Row Station, Mr. Jackson, and have done for some time."

"Oh, right, of course you would. Right then. I will leave you to it."

"Thank you." Emmy waits until he leaves before dialing out.

After a few rings, a timid voice picks up on the other end.

"Mr. Marlowe's residence."

"Lyn? Is that you?" Emmy whispers into the telephone.

"Yes?" Lyn answers.

"It's Emmy."

"Oh, Miss Nation," the relief in Lyn's voice comes through the telephone to Emmy as clear as if she were standing in front of the maid.

"I need your help this afternoon. Do you think you can get away?"

"Yes, Mr. Marlowe is out until this evening and all my work is done."

"Good. Listen, I have a big task ahead of me and I cannot plan it on my own because Colin is watching me like a hawk. I need someone who can deliver a few messages. Are you game?"

"Certainly. Should I come to you?"

"Yes, but make sure you have a reason to come. Make up a false note from Cliff that you are delivering, and I will have the other notes ready to go with their addresses and directions for you."

"I will leave shortly."

"Thanks, Lyn. I've got to run. Goodbye." Emmy hangs up the phone and rushes to place her payment on the counter. "Thank you, Mr. Jackson, I really must hurry," she says as she runs out the door.

She makes it back into her flat just as Colin rounds the corner with a paper bag full of mint leaves. She sits down, trying to collect herself, and notices all her notes are still out on her table.

"Bugger," she curses under her breath and sweeps the various papers into a pile under her bed just as a knock on her door rings out.

"Come in," she replies and Colin enters her flat with the concerned look he has been wearing since they discovered Edith was the mole.

"How are you?" he asks with so much sympathy it almost makes Emmy gag.

"I am surviving," she replies in her sickliest voice.

"You look flushed, do you have a fever?"

Emmy puts her hands to her cheeks, which are red from running. "Maybe a slight one—don't worry too much, Colin. I will be fine. Just let me rest for the day and I will be ready to take on the new one tomorrow."

"Can I make you some tea?"

"No, no, I think I will climb into bed and sleep if I can."

"I am just next door if you need me."

"I know," Emmy adds as Colin slips through the door between their flats and disappears. Now to get ready for Lyn's arrival.

When Lyn knocks on the door, Colin opens his before Emmy can make it to her own.

"What does Mr. Marlowe want now? She is sick today," he says to Lyn on the landing.

"I'm sorry, sir. I am just here to deliver this letter and then I am on my way. I do not know what it says inside."

"I will give it to her," Colin reaches out for the letter just as Emmy opens her door.

"Colin, don't be rude. I am happy to receive Lyn for a few minutes," Emmy says gently. "Hello, Lyn, why don't you come on inside and have a cuppa while I read this." Emmy takes Lyn by the arm and leads her inside. "I am a bit under the weather, but that is no reason to be impolite. I will be all right and I don't need a bodyguard."

"Of course, I am sorry." He hangs his head as she closes the door in his face.

"That man is driving me crazy," Emmy whispers to Lyn. "Ever since we discovered that Edith was the mole, he has had it in his head that we can't trust anyone and that I am going to get hurt somehow."

"He blames himself for not catching on to Edith's deception."

"Yes, I suppose. You are quite astute, Lyn," Emmy commends while putting the kettle on the stove to boil.

"Now, here are the letters I need you to deliver," she continues. "The most important one is to Miss Alice Sinclair."

"The actress?" Lyn asks, amazed.

"Yes, the actress. You will find her getting ready for a matinee performance on Shaftesbury Avenue. The address is on the envelope, but you will know the theatre by the large portrait of Georgia Ann Greenwood in the window. Go to the stage door and say you have a letter for Miss Sinclair. They should let you in, or at least deliver the letter to her dressing room for you. If they give you any trouble, you can tell them that I sent you. They know me to be one of Miss Sinclair's friends."

"Understood." Lyn takes the first letter.

"Now, the second letter is to Mrs. Williams. I have included her address and directions to her house here," Emmy passes over the letter and directions and then goes to the whistling kettle. "She won't be at home, but you can leave it for her." Emmy pours boiling water into her kettle and places it on a tray with two teacups.

"Miss, isn't Mrs. Williams in Holloway? I overheard Mr. Marlowe on the telephone discussing it."

"She is, but her husband has secured her release for tomorrow."

"I see. And the last letter?"

"It is to Flora Drummond. The address is on the envelope."

"Anything else, miss?" Lyn tucks the letters into her plain brown purse, a hand-me-down, from the looks of it.

"Can you manage it all this afternoon?"

"Yes, I think so."

"Good. These letters contain very sensitive information, Lyn. They need to be delivered to the hands of the recipients, with the exception of Mrs. Williams, of course."

"I understand, miss." Lyn's face looks grave.

"Would you like some tea?"

"Yes, please." Emmy sees Lyn relax ever so slightly.

"Tell me how Cliff is doing? Anything to report on the home front?"

"Other than being angrier than usual? Nothing. He is hurt, Miss Nation, that is clear, and he turns that hurt into anger."

"I feel terrible. I'm sorry if your life is more stressful because of me."

"I am glad that you said no. He is not a nice man. I know he has his moments, but they are really only moments with you. Most of the time, I thought he was acting the part he thought you wanted. I believe if you had married him he would have turned right back into the man you refused two years ago."

"Thank you, Lyn."

"Is that the time?" Lyn notices the clock in the corner. "I thought I had the whole day. I'd better get going on these tasks, maybe we can save the tea for another time."

"Of course." Emmy walks Lyn out and then lets out a sigh of relief. She had done the right thing.

Colin bursts into Emmy's flat after Lyn has left. He looks serious, as though he is going to tell her something tragic.

"What is it, Colin?" Emmy asks, looking up into his dark eyes.

"Emmy, what is going on?" Colin asks.

"I don't know what you mean," she tries to sound innocent.

"You are planning something. I can tell, and it is something outside of the police, which worries me."

"I am not planning anything. You are clearly reading into things too deeply," Emmy attempts to brush Colin off. How did he know that she was up to something unusual? It couldn't have been the presence of Lyn. Her argument with Cliff had only been yesterday. That wasn't enough time for news of her firing from Scotland Yard to reach Colin, was it?

"Emmy, don't lie to me," he raises his voice. Emmy looks up, shocked. Colin has never raised his voice.

"Excuse me?" she asks, anger starting to bubble. "Are you accusing me of being a liar? How dare you?" Emmy feels the hypocrisy in her words, but does not let it show on her face.

"Forgive me, Emmy, I didn't mean to offend you. It's just that we know each other rather well and I know when something is not right. It seems like things are not right now and I wish you would talk to me about them. I'm just trying to be a friend."

"Or are you trying to get information to pass on to Cliff and boost your status inside the Met?" Emmy throws the accusation back at him.

"How did you know about that?"

"It doesn't matter how, it matters that I am not sure I can trust you anymore."

"But, what about the other night, before Edith? Was that not real?"

"Of course it was real, but it doesn't negate all the other things that we have gone through. Our lives are dominated by lies and deception, Colin. It is always going to be hard for us to trust each other and know what is the truth and what is not."

"It never was so hard. We always told each other the truth before."

"Did we?"

"I certainly did and I thought you did as well. Was that also a lie?"

"I am not lying to you, Colin," Emmy sighs, feeling the truth that she is keeping inside start burning at the pit of her stomach.

"Fine, keep it to yourself then, but Emmy, be careful. Make sure whatever it is you are planning behind my back is really worth the risk. Make sure it is something you would return to Holloway for willingly, because going behind my back and behind the back of Scotland Yard, will likely end in that jail cell."

"I know what I am doing." Emmy stands up defiantly.

"Fine," Colin sighs, closing his door behind him and regretting everything that he has just said. He wants desperately to hold her in his arms and kiss her again. He wants desperately to leave London with her and have a quiet life in the country without the troubles of the Met or the WSPU. But life doesn't work that way.

Emmy locks her side of the door after he goes, wanting to be completely alone. As much as she hated what Colin just said, he was right. Is she ready for this? Ready to go back to Holloway, if that is what it comes to? She isn't sure she has a choice in the matter. She must get her mother out of London and as far away from Cliff as possible. She can think of no farther place than Canada.

❧

Hoping that Lyn has delivered her letters and everyone has completed the tasks she had asked of them, Emmy sneaks out her front door and down the stairs as quietly as she can. She does not hear anything from Colin's flat as she goes, and when she gets outside she can see his silhouette sitting at his desk through the window.

It is late, but the meeting has to happen tonight to give everyone the time to prepare their parts. Emmy walks her bike out into the street and rides away, leaving Colin at his desk.

Colin waits until Emmy goes around the side of the building for her bicycle before he follows her. He leaves the light on, in case she looks back. He had heard her sneak out and is determined to figure out what is going on. He reaches the front door in time to see her riding away. He will need a bicycle if he has any hope of following her.

It doesn't take long for Colin to find his neighbour's bike resting behind the house next door and he takes off in the same direction as Emmy had. He quickly catches up to her but keeps his distance, just enough to stay in the shadows while keeping her in his sights. It is no surprise to him when she pulls up in front of the familiar building of the WSPU headquarters. His suspicion that she is more loyal to the suffragettes than Scotland Yard starts to feel more possible.

The WSPU headquarters are abandoned except for Emmy, Alice Sinclair, her producer and fellow actress, Georgia Ann Greenwood, and two ladies that General Drummond had sent, Mrs. Sheila Fletcher and Miss Verna Daugherty. Mrs. Williams will be filled in once she is home from Holloway the following day.

"Ladies, we are here to plan a very important and top-secret mission," Emmy begins. "We have been tasked by Mrs. Pankhurst to ensure the safe boarding and departure of Mrs. Williams on her trip to Canada. She leaves the day after tomorrow. Mrs. Williams has recently been arrested, but her husband has managed to secure her bail. However, several stipulations were put on her, including a prohibition from leaving the city of London or participating in any private or public suffrage activities. But, most importantly, she is to be chaperoned at all times. Obviously, these prove to be quite the obstacles in arranging for Mrs. Williams to get to Canada. Which is why you are all here."

"You have a plan of some sort, I assume," Georgia Ann says with her usual condescension.

"Yes, at least the shell of one, and hopefully this evening we can fill it all out."

"What do you propose, Emmy?" Alice gives Emmy a reassuring smile.

Emmy looks around the small circle of women. What she has planned is dangerous and, in her opinion, could use another month of careful thinking through. But despite the nausea growing in her stomach, she doesn't have a choice. She has to move forward.

"I have arranged for a ticket for the boat under the name of Vera Gilbert. Vera Gilbert does not exist, but I have General Drummond working on securing false documentation for her to prove she is a Canadian citizen on her way home. This will be Mrs. Williams' alias and she will need a clever disguise to fool any police with her image in hand. That is where Alice and Miss Greenwood come in. We need something that will really fool them, ladies. Vera Gilbert will not be travelling in style, to put it delicately, so her clothing will need to be quite different from her usual attire. I am also thinking that a wig is likely in order, and perhaps some special makeup, to really sell it."

"I can add some wrinkles to make her look a bit older, and we can give her a dark wig and fill in her eyebrows to match," Alice suggests.

"How far do you want us to go with this, Emmy?" Georgia Ann cuts in.

"It should be natural. We don't want to draw attention to Vera Gilbert at all. She just needs to look as far from Mrs. Williams as possible. Alice is right, Mrs. Williams has blonde hair, so we should give her a dark wig, and add some wrinkles to make her look more worn. Maybe a pair of spectacles. The rest can be done with costuming. No one should look too closely at a third-class passenger when they are looking for a rich, elegant woman travelling with her husband. Which reminds me, Mr. Williams was planning on travelling to Canada with his wife. He will still be going, presumably alone. That will help draw the attention away from Vera Gilbert."

"This is quite complicated," Sheila adds. "How do we get Vera Gilbert, or Mrs. Williams, out of her house without being followed?"

"Yes, this is going to be the hardest part," Emmy sighs. "I've thought a lot about this and it will be a multi-part plan. To begin with, Mrs. Williams arrives home from Holloway tomorrow. She will send out invitations for a small tea party to her closest friends. That will be the four of us. Miss Daugherty is already established as the housekeeper for the Williams family. Now, Mrs. Fletcher, Miss Daugherty, Miss Greenwood, I am going to let you in on a secret that I have kept for some time. Alice already knows and so do the WSPU leaders. I am trusting you with my life here, and only because I trust all of you explicitly am I sharing this information. I am a double agent. The Metropolitan Police Force believe that I am a mole inside the WSPU passing information back to them. In reality, my loyalties lie here, with you, and I deceive the Met as much as I can."

"You what?!" Georgia Ann shrieks. "You work for the enemy? I knew something fishy was happening with you and Mr. Marlowe. How do we know that you are loyal to us and not to them? Is this all a set-up?"

"Georgia, calm down." Alice grabs her overly dramatic friend by the shoulders. "Emmy is on our side, trust me, I know. You can relax and take a breath."

"How do you know you can trust her, Alice?"

"Because I've helped her before and she is good to her word."

"What about Mr. Marlowe?" Georgia Ann turns back to Emmy.

"Mr. Marlowe is a means to an end, Miss Greenwood, and nothing more."

"But he asked you to marry him?"

"I'm sorry to interrupt what is clearly a personal matter," Verna Daugherty speaks between Georgia Ann and Emmy, "but, this is quite a lot to take in. Please explain."

Emmy takes a deep breath and explains her story from the day she was asked to go undercover as a suffragette to this point.

"You were sent here by General Drummond, which is why I have trusted you with this information. Ask yourselves, if she trusted me with this mission, can you?" Emmy adds in conclusion.

"I don't see why not," Sheila replies. "It is clear that Mrs. Pankhurst and Mrs. Drummond rely on you for many things."

"Agreed," Verna echoes. "If they trust you, then so do I."

"Georgia Ann?" Alice looks to the actress.

"Well, I don't see that I have much choice, do I?"

"Miss Greenwood, I asked you to come tonight because you are one of the greatest actresses in London and we need the performance of a lifetime to pull this scheme off. You have given so much to the suffrage movement already, if you are not able to give this, we will all understand." Emmy keeps her eyes steady on Georgia Ann but can see Alice shake her head off to the side. Emmy has played right into Georgia Ann's ego and Alice watches with a smile as the diva falls into the trap.

"Of course I am willing to do this for the WSPU. I am devoutly loyal to the cause. What do you need from me, other than costumes?"

"You will all be invited to Mrs. Williams' home for tea. I will convince my superiors at Scotland Yard that I can get myself an invitation as Alice's guest, in order to keep tabs on Mrs. Williams and make sure the tea party is not a suffrage meeting. Once we arrive, the work begins. Mrs. Williams will be disguised as one of us and she will take our place on the way out. Leaving one of us behind to pretend to be Mrs. Williams until she is safely on her way to Canada. Miss Greenwood, this is what I need you to do."

"You want me to impersonate Mrs. Williams? For how long? I have things to do you know."

"I know, it will only be for a few days. Just long enough for the boat to get safely into the Atlantic and away from the shores of England. You are the only one talented enough to do this. It must be a complete deception, even from her servants."

"How am I to deceive her lady's maid?"

"Due to the fact that they are going on such a long journey, Mrs. Williams' lady's maid and several other servants left two days ago on an earlier boat, to allow them time to get the house in Toronto established before the Williamses arrive. Fortunately for us, Miss Daugherty will be taking care of Mrs. Williams in place of her lady's maid. The household has been running on a temporary staff and they will all be let go for a vacation when the Williamses depart. Miss Daugherty, the butler, and two others will be the only remaining servants while the Williamses are in Canada. However, you are encouraged to remain indoors and perhaps contract some sort of illness to keep you in bed and not receiving visitors. Mrs. Williams has been on hunger strike, so an illness will not be a stretch. We need to avoid engagement with the chaperone at all costs. The butler has been bribed by the court into being the chaperone, so the more inappropriate it is for him to see Miss Greenwood up close, the better."

"How will we explain Mr. Williams going without his wife?" Verna asks.

"Mr. Williams has been a long-time supporter of the WSPU and women's suffrage. He will be taking the place of Mrs. Williams on her speaking tour."

"When does she turn into Vera Gilbert?" Alice asks.

"Once we have Mrs. Williams out of the house, she will return to the theatre, where Miss Greenwood would likely go. From there we can dress her up as Vera and she can leave for the train to Southampton, hopefully with no prying eyes from the Met. Once she is on the train, she is out of our purview. The Southampton suffrage organization will take over from there."

"Sounds like a solid plan." Alice pats Emmy on the shoulder. "Great work, darling."

"Thank you. Any questions?"

"I don't think so." Sheila looks around with an eyebrow raised. "It all seems fairly clear. All we do now is wait for the invitations?"

"Yes. Sheila, your part is mainly that of friend and supporter to Mrs. Williams. We know that you are already close to her as it is, so this should seem natural. You will help sell the deception of the tea party and then you can visit Miss Greenwood if we feel we need to solidify the scheme at all."

"Understood."

"Verna, you will fill in Mr. and Mrs. Williams when they return from Holloway in the morning. I have also sent a letter with a few details, and Mrs. Drummond will be sending the false documentation in the morning."

"Yes, of course."

"Alice, Miss Greenwood, we need to get these disguises in order. Shall we go to the theatre?"

"We have a show in an hour. We can work through the intermission." Alice tosses her cashmere wrap around her shoulders.

"Thank you, all," Emmy finishes off. "We shall see each other for tea."

As everyone leaves the offices, Alice pulls Emmy aside. "Do you think it wise to include Georgia Ann in this?"

"I think it wiser than keeping her out of it. It would be worse if she discovered this plot and felt left out, don't you think?"

"I suppose you are right. I just hope she can keep her mind off her performance and on the actual task at hand."

"Me, too."

Colin watches as five ladies leave the building. He doesn't recognize the first two, but he certainly knows the other three. Alice Sinclair and Georgia Ann Greenwood are not inconspicuous company for Emmy to be keeping. Even a washer woman who has never been to the theatre would know who they were if she passed them on the street. What has Emmy gotten herself into?

CHAPTER 12

July 19, 1913

COLIN ARRIVES HOME FROM a morning spent at Cannon Row Station reviewing Mrs. Williams' case, to find Emmy with a note from Alice Sinclair in her hand.

"How was your morning?" she asks, trying to sound normal after their heated discussion the other day.

"Marlowe said he suspended you," Colin replies, trying to hide how hurt he feels that Emmy had kept that to herself.

"Oh, yes, the suspension. We got in a little fight and well, he decided to take it out on me professionally," Emmy tries to make it sound less severe than it was.

"You got in a fight? A personal fight?" Colin does the prodding now. He had kissed Emmy, he had finally made his feelings clear, and she had gone back to Marlowe?

"Well, yes. Actually, I told him that I couldn't..." Emmy stops. She hadn't told Colin about Cliff's proposal, should she now? "I told him that I did not want to see him outside of work anymore. Not after what happened between us." Emmy smiles at Colin. They had barely spoken of that night. The shock of Edith's deception had overshadowed the kiss that came before it. Now the awkwardness fills the space and leaves the two of them searching for words.

"Marlowe is putting together a team to prevent Mrs. Williams from leaving for her tour of Canada. Her husband has managed her release from Holloway and Marlowe is determined to do everything in his power to stop her from leaving the country," Colin says, returning to work-related topics and safe territory.

"Well, I may just be able to help you with that. I received an invitation from Alice to join her and Miss Greenwood. They have been invited to tea at Mrs. Williams' this afternoon and Alice asks, won't I please join her so she 'might have decent company with which to buffer the boringness of the event?'" Emmy reads out.

"Well, this is perfect! Mr. Marlowe has asked that we keep our eyes on Mrs. Williams and make sure she does not attempt to get on the train to Southampton and now we have a way inside her house," Colin exclaims.

"It is very convenient." Emmy questions, "Do you think anything fishy is going on?"

"You know Miss Sinclair—does it seem like fishy behaviour to you?"

"Not at all, it seems quite normal for Miss Sinclair."

"Well, that is your answer then," Colin replies simply, though it did, in fact, seem fishy to him that Miss Sinclair had made their assignment from Marlowe that much easier.

"I suppose. I should respond to this letter so Alice does not fret too much," Emmy replies, pinning her hat in place.

"Of course. I will see you back here? I should go over a few things with you about this case."

"What about my suspension?"

"This is our best way inside, so we can tell Marlowe about it after we have results," Colin lies. He needs to know how this whole thing will play out. He needs to find out what Emmy is up to behind his back.

"I will quickly run to the post office and send a telegram to Alice," Emmy replies as she races out the door. *The plan is in place and all seems to be going well*, she thinks with a secret smile to herself.

Emmy enters the post office on the corner and walks straight to the counter.

"I need to send a telegram to Miss Sinclair in Shaftesbury Avenue, please, Mr. Jackson."

"Yes, Miss Nation. Write it out here." Mr. Jackson hands Emmy a piece of paper.

Received invitation. Plan is a go. Em

"Excellent, I will send it right away."

Emmy completes the transaction and begins for home swiftly to continue the work with Colin, hoping that he won't suspect how lucky it all was turning out to be.

But Colin did suspect something. He had been more alert to Emmy's actions and movements since her visit with Lyn a few days earlier, and their heated discussion afterwards. Colin had been on the lookout for suspicious activity from Emmy, and he was seeing signs pointing to something dubious everywhere. He wasn't sure how he was going to prove it, or if he even wanted to prove it. If Emmy was going behind the Met and working fully for the WSPU, that was cause for imprisonment. She could be charged with a serious offence, even treason. Did he want to be the one to report her? Although, if he was the one to report on the activity, he could downplay Emmy's role, protecting her from too strict a charge and accompanying punishment.

"What the devil could she be up to?" he asks the empty room, trying to think about the WSPU's recent activities. When it dawns on him, he cannot believe how blind he has been. Of course, she was part of getting Mrs. Williams to the boat. She had met with Lyn the same day that Cliff had given him the assignment, and then she had gone out that night to a secret meeting of suffragettes that she claimed was part of something else, but at least two of the women at that meeting were going to Mrs. Williams' house today with Emmy. All fingers pointed to this one event. The timing was too conspicuous for it not to be.

"Damn it, Emmy," Colin swears. How could she put him in this position?

He begins to draft his own telegram but he will have to wait until Emmy goes to tea to send it. He will pretend to have received a tip, from a trusted source that did not want to officially come forward, that Mrs. Williams and the WSPU are planning to try to get her on the boat as scheduled. He will ask for a few extra men to help him patrol the docks and Mrs. Williams' house. If all goes well, he will arrest Mrs. Williams in the act and not spot Emmy anywhere during the entire event. If all goes well, and Marlowe trusts him.

Emmy arrives outside Mrs. Williams' house for the second time in her life. The first time, she had been rushing in after her first reunion with Cliff at Cannon Row Station. They had fought, and she had been forced to deceive Colin to keep her history a secret. She had been late arriving to the house and Edith was running around like a madwoman trying to get food for the party organized in time. She had not been pleased with Emmy's tardiness.

Today, Emmy arrives right on time. She is hardly ever late anymore, primarily because Colin goes most places with her and he always insists on being early, so he can stake out a good place to wait and keep his eye on her. She looks across the street to where she knows he is sitting on a bench reading a newspaper. She had fallen in love with him, but things had changed. Her life had changed, her priorities had changed, and now he was more of a bother to her than a pleasure to be with. Still, she was in love with him. If only things were simpler, she would tell him all her secrets and ask him to move to the Rose Garden Cottage with her so they could live a simple life together.

She had managed to slip away to say a final goodbye to her mother after Colin had gone to sleep the previous night. It had been a tearful meeting, the two women not knowing when they would see each other again, and Emmy had felt the weight and sadness of her life pressing down on her since she left the train station. But, when Colin peeks up over the paper and sees Emmy looking at him, she smiles. He smiles back, cheeks reddening as they always do when Emmy smiles at him, and returns to reading so they won't draw attention to each other.

Emmy knocks on the door. Edith will not be with her this time. Edith will never be with her again. Even if they do rekindle their friendship, Edith's time in the WSPU is over. Her husband has made sure of that.

Suddenly Emmy feels very cold, very alone. She has Alice, Georgia Ann, Sheila, and Verna, but she is without her two closest confidants and friends. Yes, Colin is close by, but he is not really with her anymore. Her deception has gone too far to count him as a close ally, even if he doesn't know that yet. He will find out though, Emmy is sure of it. Colin is a smart man and he has figured out her secrets before, so he is bound to figure them out a second time.

Mrs. Williams' butler answers the door and leads Emmy into the drawing room where all the other ladies, including Mrs. Williams, have already gathered.

"Oh, Emmy, I simply cannot believe that you want me to play the part of Mrs. Williams here, in this house, for two days," Georgia Ann greets her, once the butler has left the room.

"Georgia, we have already discussed this and you agreed to the plan. You cannot back out now," Emmy panics.

"Sweetie, no, I wouldn't dream of it. I simply meant that this house is quite possibly the most divine thing

I've ever been inside. I feel dreadful to be the sole person privileged to be given this part in our scheme. Here I will be, lounging in the lap of luxury, relaxing in the seat of opulence and comfort, eating delicious foods, and relishing in the richness of this marvellous home, while the rest of you are out wearing itchy wigs and pretending to be servant girls in order to sneak poor Mrs. Williams into a third-class boat cabin. I feel far too lucky to have snagged this part." Georgia Ann emotes all this while gliding around the drawing room as if she were on stage in front of an audience of five hundred instead of five. To punctuate the end of her monologue, she tosses the long silk scarf she has been holding in both hands over her shoulder, covering her décolletage in the bright yellow fabric that contrasts against her vibrant blue dress.

"Well, you are the only actress capable of such a role," Emmy plays into her, giving Alice a wink at the same time.

"That is right, Georgia," Alice plays along. "I could not pull it off myself. Only you, darling. Now, can we get to business?"

"Don't let me hold you back; I need to witness Mrs. Williams in her natural state so I may imitate her physicality and speaking mannerisms. Don't mind me, I will be over in the corner here. Mrs. Williams, just be yourself and pretend that I am not here at all."

"Of course." Mrs. Williams smiles politely at the actress. "Thank you, Miss Greenwood, and to all of you for being here to help me get to Canada." She sits elegantly near the fireplace in a manner Emmy remembers from her childhood. Only a proper lady sits so perfectly while still looking at ease. A task her own mother had spent countless hours working on with Emmy.

Mrs. Williams sips her tea with a steady hand, despite having just come from the horrors of Holloway. Emmy notices that her eyes also betray no sense of nervousness about the task at hand. Mrs. Williams is calm and collected. Her blonde hair is speckled with grey and wrinkles have formed around her eyes, but otherwise she looks strong and capable, not the frail, middle-aged woman Emmy was expecting.

"We do have work to do, Mrs. Williams. Has the plan been explained to you?" Emmy asks.

"Yes, Sheila and Verna let me know all the details."

"Excellent, then we are ready to get started. We need to get you changed into your disguise."

"Right. Mr. Williams is overseeing the last of his packing for the trip and I have sent my maid out for some medicine for my cold. We should have an hour at most to get this done."

"Just enough time for a tea party," Emmy grins.

Mrs. Williams leads the ladies upstairs to her dressing room and they all help change her out of her own clothes and into the clothes that Georgia Ann wore to the party, dressing Georgia Ann back up as Mrs. Williams. The wigs that Alice brought in her larger-than-normal, but not so large to draw attention, purse complete the transformation. Georgia Ann had been clever to wear a hat with a veil on it, so Mrs. Williams' face will be hidden on her way out.

"Lucky thing we are the same height and size, Mrs. Williams, wouldn't you say?" Georgia Ann runs her hands over the silk dress she has appropriated from her muse.

"Yes, lucky thing." Mrs. Williams looks back at Emmy, knowingly. It was no mistake on Emmy's part that Georgia Ann was picked over Alice to do this task. Alice was almost a foot taller than Mrs. Williams and quite a bit fuller in the bosom. The two would never have been able to swap clothing so seamlessly.

"This dress does feel wonderful. Who is your dressmaker? I simply must have her name." Georgia Ann's focus is still firmly planted on herself in the mirror.

"I shall leave it for you with Miss Sinclair. Now, we must be off, right, Miss Nation?"

"Right. Tea time has come to an end, I believe. Verna and Sheila, you will stay here with Georgia Ann and inform the maid about her bedrest when she returns. You can take the medicine up to her. It will be up to you two to take care of our dear Mrs. Williams."

"Of course, up to bed we go," Sheila directs Georgia Ann. "And, good luck to you all."

"Say hello to my cousin, Joan, in Toronto, will you?" Verna asks, giving Mrs. Williams a quick hug.

"Of course. Be safe. I will write to you as soon as I can."

"All right, we three are on our way to the theatre. Shall we?" Emmy gestures towards the door.

"Are you set, Mrs. Williams?" Alice asks.

"I am as ready as I ever will be." Mrs. Williams pulls the veil over her calm face, almost as though she had long ago accepted her fate and was happy to meet whatever life gave to her with proper English manners and grace.

"Anchors away, as they say." Emmy takes the new Georgia Ann by the arm and leads her out of the posh house.

Mrs. Williams had directed her chauffeur to drive her guests back to the theatre. The shiny black motor car is pulled up in front of the house, waiting for the ladies. As they climb in, Emmy sees the two uniformed police constables at the corner watching them, as well as a familiar plain clothes detective on the bench across from Colin. Privy to Emmy's plan to return to the theatre with the actresses, Colin is already getting up and starting the walk towards the theatre district, where he will meet her when she is done. Emmy watches out the window to see if any of the other police officers follow them, but only Colin makes a move. Clearly, the first part of the deception has succeeded.

Colin begins to follow the motor car with a heavy heart. He had sent his telegram while Emmy was having her tea, and he is certain that Marlowe will take immediate action and gather as many men as he has on hand. Emmy's plan will fail; he is sure of it. He just isn't sure if he can save her in the process.

CHAPTER 13

July 19, 1913

THE MOTOR CAR PULLS up at the stage door entrance to Georgia Ann's theatre and the ladies giggle and gossip their way inside, hoping to fool the doorman with so much chatter that he will not notice anything out of place with his boss. Fortunately, Jeffrey is always slightly drunk and, in the middle of a day with no shows, he is currently half asleep.

"Jeffrey," Alice tips her hat to him as they pass and gets nothing more than a grunt in return. The three of them sign in and mark the time. Alice forges Georgia Ann's signature to perfection.

In Alice's dressing room, the real magic begins.

"Here is your next costume, Mrs. Williams," Alice pulls out a shabby, rough cotton dress with an overcoat, all in various shades of brown.

"Where can I change?"

"Just behind this curtain here. Let me know if you need any help getting out of Georgia Ann's dress."

"You should remove the wig first, I should think," Emmy adds.

"Ah, yes, I had almost forgotten about it. They are not as uncomfortable as I had imagined." Mrs. Williams hands the wig to Alice and steps behind the curtain.

"I think we might need to adjust your dialect slightly, Mrs. Williams. Your voice doesn't quite fit your outfit."

"I would have to agree with you, Miss Sinclair," Mrs. Williams replies from behind the curtain.

While Alice runs through some basics for Mrs. Williams, to make her speech sound less like an upper-class Lady, Emmy peeks out from the corner of the window and sees the alley is empty.

"It looks like we may have succeeded. I don't see anyone out there."

"That's good news," Mrs. Williams tries out the sentence with her new accent as she emerges from the curtain in a brown dress with a patched-up overcoat to match.

"That sounds pretty good, Mrs. Williams. You are a quick study," Emmy is happily surprised.

"Hopefully, I won't have to say too much. I fear I couldn't keep it going for longer than a few words. See, I have already slipped back into my normal voice."

"Let us get the makeup on and ready and then we can return to the dialect issue, shall we?"

"Ready when you are." Mrs. Williams sits in the chair by the makeup table.

"Are you excited for your tour of Canada, Mrs. Williams?" Alice changes the subject while she begins working on the hair and makeup for the disguise.

"I am excited to see the country and the vastness of it. It sounds quite remarkable. Although, I have to admit that I am rather worried about the company."

"How so?" Alice prods.

"It is just that some of these Canadian suffragists, like their American counterparts, are really quite, well, how to put this nicely... They are not quite as open and accepting to women of various ethnicities as the circle I associate with here in London. Not to say that we British are all veritable examples of inclusion and acceptance. In fact, I find our organization and others here in England to be some of the worst propagators of prejudice in our society, but I no longer choose to associate with the suffragists here that are firmly against the inclusion of women from different races in our cause. And I have been using my status within the WSPU to start to undermine some of these attitudes inside the organization as well. The women that I am to be hosted by in Canada are very much openly against inclusion of all women in their campaign. It is almost as though they are choosing, politically, to ally themselves with men of power strictly through the whiteness of their skin. A notion that I have moved far beyond and I am hoping to convince them to as well."

"I suppose they have a variety of different opinions across the ocean and different ways of viewing their world than we do," Alice adds, looking happily at the transformation she has created. "We should send them Edy Craig and Christabel Marshall—they may never recover from that shock," Alice smiles.

"Better we should send them your playwrights, Elizabeth Robins and Bernard Shaw. Like them, there are many eugenicists in Canada, and I fear I may not be able to handle it. Thank goodness Mr. Williams will be with me."

"Oh dear, I am so sorry, Mrs. Williams. Perhaps you are just who they need to show them the path. Are you all right?"

"What's wrong?" Emmy asks when she sees Mrs. Williams' face cloud over with sorrow.

"I had a daughter. We had a daughter, Mr. Williams and I did. It's funny, I do that all the time. Call her mine and not ours. I suppose loss has a way of making you feel totally alone in your pain, even when the person beside you has lost the very same thing. Our daughter was born beautiful and imperfect to the eyes of the world. But to us, she was the most perfect thing we had ever seen. When she laughed... Well, she was considered to be a weak link in the evolutionary chain. When she died, when her heart finally gave out at the age of five, I was exhausted. We had spent her entire life fighting with doctors who wanted to take her away from us and put her in an institution. We never let them take her. We brought in nurses to be with her every hour of the day. They were all Nightingales, the best nurses in London.

Many of my friends were believers in the eugenics movement and I had never given it much thought. It was only later on, when the emotional fog of everything we had been through had lifted and I began to read more about women's rights and think more deeply about the situation, that I understood the horror of eugenics. My daughter, Diana, was perfect, in her own way, just as she was. Had she grown to a full woman, I would have supported her every choice, including having her own life and family."

"Mrs. Williams," Emmy places her hand over the older woman's. "I am so very sorry."

"For now, we are focused on earning our right to vote, but once we achieve that, I will be putting all my attention into fighting for more rights for women of all walks of life, not just those who share my specific place in society. And for rights over our bodies. We deserve to make the choices for ourselves. I will fight in her memory for the rights she would have been denied had she grown up."

"We know you will, Mrs. Williams, and I will be beside you in that fight," Alice squeezes her other hand.

"As will I," Emmy pledges.

"Enough of this blubbering now, ladies. We have a mission to complete. How are we looking, Miss Nation?" Mrs. Williams wipes away her tears.

Emmy goes to the window overlooking the back alley. She pulls the drapes back ever so slightly and peeks out.

"Did we have anyone follow us?" Alice inquires.

"Not from here. Where can I get a good look out to Shaftesbury Avenue?"

"Just across the corridor, the last door on the left. It should be unlocked," Alice says.

Emmy walks down the empty hallway and opens the last door on the left. She enters what must be Georgia Ann's office. It is small and rather cramped, not quite what she had envisioned for a woman of Georgia Ann's large character. Yet, it is lavishly decorated in bright colours and ostentatious furniture. A small wooden desk sits in the centre of the room, on top of a leopard rug and flanked by two chairs draped in silk fabric of various shades of green, orange, and purple. The artwork is gaudy, to say the least, and suits the over-the-top personality of the actress quite nicely. Underneath all of this show, Emmy sees that the office is older and only a small little corner carved out of storage space in the cramped backstage area of the building. Georgia Ann Greenwood may be outrageously over the top, but that did not mean her budget was. Considering her position as one of only a few women theatre producers in all of London who rented her own theatre on Shaftesbury Avenue, Emmy conceded that she likely did not live the way she presented herself to. Emmy understands perfectly where she is coming from. She had been in the same position just months earlier, hiding the holes in her boots and the emptiness of her stomach from everyone around her.

Emmy spots the only window in the place, a tiny opening not much bigger than a porthole in a ship. The sunlight shining through the narrow slit in the drapes illuminates the dust floating around Georgia Ann's desk. Emmy moves slowly and stays out of the rays of light. If someone is watching them from below, she does not want to draw attention to herself.

She reaches the window and takes up the same position as she did in Alice's dressing room. Peeking out from a tiny hole in the curtains, she quickly spots Colin on the street corner. Only, he isn't alone.

Emmy watches as Colin talks to two uniformed police constables and a plain clothes detective. They are the same ones that had been waiting outside Mrs. Williams' house.

"Bugger," she swears at the room and keeps watching. Colin points to the theatre and then to the side street that will lead to the back alley with the stage door. The plain clothes detective moves in that direction and Emmy watches as he disappears around the corner.

"Bloody hell," she rushes out of the office and back to Alice's dressing room.

"Ladies, we may not have been as successful as we thought," Emmy barges in.

"What is happening?" Alice asks.

"It's Colin." Emmy sits, devastated. "I knew he would find me out eventually, but I had no idea it had already happened. He must have overheard my conversation with Lyn the other day, or followed her, or followed me," Emmy's voice reaches a higher pitch with every realization.

"Emmy, Emmy, listen to me." Alice crouches in front of her friend. "We do not know anything for certain. Just take a deep breath and calm down. We cannot stay here, we must still get Mrs. Williams to the boat. Collect yourself and your emotions, we can be mad at Colin after this is all done. Here." Alice begins to pour brandy from the crystal bar set she has on her makeup table. "Drink this." She hands Emmy a snifter full of the amber liquid. "Mrs. Williams, would you care for a brandy?"

"Oh, yes, please, I can think of nothing better at this moment," Mrs. Williams replies.

"Ok," Emmy says after taking a large sip of her brandy. "Ok, we have to move forward," she adds, to reassure herself more than the others. She goes back to the window and peers outside. The plain clothes detective is standing across the alley, subtly keeping his eye on the stage door.

"So, it looks like we will have company on the way out." Emmy tries to regain command of herself and the situation. "Detective on guard in the alley and Colin, plus two uniforms, out front."

"Well, we shall have to outplay them. Don't worry, Mrs. Williams, you have two of the best on your team. Isn't that right, Emmy?"

"Yes, that is right," Emmy uses the words to convince herself just as much as Mrs. Williams. "We will need to leave without you, I fear, Mrs. Williams. I believe that it is best if Alice and I try to draw the police away with us. I highly doubt they have any suspicion of Georgia Ann Greenwood being in league with us. She has never made any public declaration of her connection with the WSPU, or the suffrage movement, for that matter."

"And she does often stay late working in her office alone. She really is quite dedicated to the theatre," Alice adds.

"Then it is settled. Mrs. Williams will stay behind. We will get your disguise finished here before we leave. You will have to wait until we get the police to follow us away from the theatre. Then, Vera Gilbert has to get out, unseen by the police and the doorman," Emmy works through the situation out loud even though she is not looking for input from her counterparts. "Alice, we should go someplace public."

"What about your friend, Gwen?" Alice asks.

"What about her?"

"Isn't her engagement party this afternoon? It is supposed to be the social event of the season."

"She is having an engagement party today? Oh, she is having an engagement party today!" Emmy remembers. "I already have an invitation. I completely forgot about it.

That would be a very public place. It is settled then. How is the makeup coming along?"

"Almost done here. Just filling in the eyebrows to match the wig, and Vera Gilbert is ready to go."

"Perfect. Mrs. Williams, as soon as you see the man in the back alley leave, you go fast. Keep your head down."

"Understood. Alice, do you have a service door, other than the stage door? Perhaps I should be using that. Where do the cleaners for the theatre come and go from?" Mrs. Williams asks.

"They use the stage door, too, but, come to think of it, we have a few secret doors in here. Including one that will get you to the theatre next door."

"What? Alice, that is huge, why didn't you mention it?" Emmy almost yells the words at her friend.

"I forgot, we never use it. I think it is covered by several layers of backdrops and set pieces."

"Well, let's go take a look. What is happening at the theatre next door?"

"Nothing. I think they are closed."

"Let's go." Emmy downs the rest of her brandy in one gulp and gestures for Alice to lead the way. The other two ladies copy her drinking technique and leave the dressing room.

They go down the stairs, all the way to the orchestra level inside the theatre. At the very back of the seats, Alice pushes open a wall panel to reveal a tiny hallway.

"That way will take you back up to the lobby," Alice points in the opposite direction. "Be careful, these stairs are quite steep."

Alice leads them down a set of old wooden stairs that are steep enough to almost be a ladder. At the bottom, they find themselves in the basement of the basement. The very bottom of the theatre that is used for storage and things to be forgotten about in dark corners. Set pieces loom around them and masks peek out from under white sheets. Alice lights a lantern that hangs at the entrance.

"See why I didn't remember this?"

"Yes, I do. When was the last time someone was down here?" Emmy asks.

"I don't know. The stagehands are convinced that a ghost lives here and they refuse to come down. At least since Georgia Ann took it over. I don't know what the feeling about the place was before that, but certainly, no one who works here has any warm feelings for the place."

"Is it haunted, Alice?" Mrs. Williams looks frightened.

"All theatres are haunted, if you ask the people who work in them. But it is simply theatrics, my dear Mrs. Williams. Even from the stagehands. All a bunch of over-dramatic babies, if you ask me. But keep close anyways, we only have this small light."

The three women grab a hold of each other and start moving slowly through the dank basement. The light casts eerie shadows across the walls and gives the impression of sheets moving as they pass.

"No ghosts, no ghosts," Mrs. Williams repeats to herself.

"How far is it, Alice?" Emmy shudders at the thought of staying in here any longer than needed.

"Just up here—see where the backdrops are all piled up?" Alice points a few feet ahead.

"Do you think we can move them?"

"I think it is our safest and best bet."

Alice places the lantern on a nearby table and the women begin hauling rolls of heavy canvas out of the way of the door.

"God, these are heavy," Alice groans, swiping at an unseen cobweb in front of her face.

"Let me grab the other end," Mrs. Williams offers. A cloud of dust bursts up as they lift, making Alice cough and Mrs. Williams scrunch her face as though she were eating a lemon.

"They smell terrible, like mould," Mrs. Williams says.

Emmy grabs a whole roll herself and tosses it aside, holding her breath so she doesn't smell them or breathe in the dust.

"What?" she questions, when Alice and Mrs. Williams stare at her in disbelief. "I train a lot. Have you met Colin? It is constant with him. We train every bloody morning, despite my protests. I've built up some arm muscles in the process. He really is rather ruthless, the bugger."

"Well, I say, Miss Nation. We shall have to enter you in the travelling circus as the strongwoman act," Alice jokes.

"Oh, come off it. I keep thinking I see a shadow out of the corner of my eye. Let's just work fast and get out of this horrid place." Emmy looks tentatively around her before picking up another roll.

In a matter of minutes, the trio free the door. With a turn of the handle, they come up against a solid force preventing them from going any further.

"It's locked," Alice cries. "We did all of that for nothing."

"Let me handle the lock." Emmy kneels, pulling her trusty hair pin out from the back of her bun. "Shine the light down here, will you, Alice?"

"Of course. Now, we shall have to call you the master burglar and the strongwoman."

"Well, I was a bit of a mischievous child and frequently picked the locks on my father's study and my mother's private rooms, but Colin has shown me a much more efficient method. He really has taught me most everything I know about all this deception and sneaking-around business. I feel rather guilty going behind his back like this," Emmy chats while working to help her hands stay steady.

"He'll understand in the end," Alice assures.

"Are you and Colin involved, Miss Nation?" Mrs. Williams asks.

"No," Emmy sighs, and Alice gives Mrs. Williams a look that explains it all.

"Ah, I see. Well, the future is never set."

"I suppose not. Got it." Emmy stands up and tries the door again. It clicks open, but requires some effort still to allow them enough space to pass, rusty hinges and all.

"Alice, do you know the way on this end?"

"Follow our noses?" she smiles.

"Better than nothing at all," Emmy shrugs.

They venture into another dark passageway and follow it along until they reach a door. Opening that with considerably more ease than the last door, Alice cautiously wraps her head around to see what is on the other side.

"All clear." She gestures to move forward. "I think we've found the matching pair," she adds pointing to a set of stairs that look identical to the ones they just descended.

"Up and out, ladies," Alice directs them up the stairs.

At the top, they find a similar hallway that leads them to a hidden door inside the theatre. Only this time, they are in the lobby, not the orchestra level. Luckily, it is deserted.

"We did it!"

"Let's find the stage door," Emmy instructs.

Working their way through the familiar layout of a theatre, the women find the stage door. It is far enough away from the watching detective to provide a clear getaway for Mrs. Williams.

"Now what?"

"Now, Alice and I have to go back through that horrid place and make our way to Gwen's party. Mrs. Williams wait here and watch until you see us leave. We will make sure to draw the attention of the detective our way, giving you a clear path to go in the opposite direction. Then, blend in and head to the train station," Emmy explains.

"Understood. Good luck and thank you." Mrs. Williams gives Emmy a hug. Her body feels strong and firm, unlike Emmy's, which is trembling slightly. She shows no hint of fear to the outside eye and Emmy takes comfort in that.

"And to you, Mrs. Williams. I will see you at the station, even if you don't see me. Back to the dungeons, Alice."

"Ladies," Mrs. Williams stops them. "You might want to take a moment to change into something a bit more appropriate."

Emmy and Alice look down at their clothes that are now covered in dust and grime.

"Good advice," Emmy says, pulling a cobweb out of Alice's hair.

"We will have to raid my wardrobe again," Alice adds with a smile. "Goodbye, Mrs. Williams."

Alice leads the way back down and through the dark passageways. The two walk in silence, holding each other around the waist and keeping their eyes peeled for ghosts. When they finally reach the back of the orchestra level again, they both exhale deeply, releasing the fear they had been holding back throughout their journey.

"Thank goodness. That was most unpleasant," Alice sighs.

"Very, very unpleasant. Let's get ready for a party"

"What I wouldn't give for a glass of champagne right now," Alice says while brushing dust off Emmy's shoulders and repinning a stray piece of hair.

"Well, Miss Sinclair, you are going to get one." Emmy hooks arms with her friend and heads to the dressing rooms.

They work quickly so that Mrs. Williams will have time to make it to her train. Luckily, Alice is used to changing costumes quickly and manages to get herself and Emmy all fixed up in a matter of minutes. Emmy is surprised at how good they look. Their hair is an elegant combination of relaxed and polished, giving their faces the perfect frames for the subtle makeup that Alice seemed to throw on, but that looks flawless. Emmy has never worn makeup before, so she is shocked at how it brightens her complexion and makes her lips stand out ever so slightly in a soft pink pucker. Alice wears the olive-green dress that she used for Hypatia, but she gave Emmy her pick and Emmy chose a dress she has had her eye on for weeks. It is a soft grey with a scoop neckline and flowing cap sleeves. The main dress is covered in a delicate lace that collects at the waist before softly flowing out and ending just below her knees. The waist is a wide ribbon, which gives the dress a refined look. To top it all off, Alice hands Emmy a pair of white satin gloves that reach up to above her elbows.

"Ready to cause a scene?" Emmy asks as they head to the stage door.

"Wait," Alice looks in the mirror hanging by the wall and checks her appearance one last time. "Ready," she nods. "What kind of scene do you want? Angry, flirtatious, damsel in distress?"

"I'd say flirtatious, that will really throw him off. Bamboozle our dear old detective, Miss Sinclair, and give our pal Vera Gilbert a good long time to get away."

"You got it." Alice bats her eyelashes at Emmy in classic coquette fashion.

On the street outside, Alice falls into the role of the flirtatious actress. The stereotype was a well-known one in London, and one that some actresses were all too eager to promote. Alice was not normally one of them, but she falls into the role easily enough. To be flirted with by a famous, gorgeous actress, even one you were assigned to watch like hawk, was enough to throw most men off their guard, and this detective was no different. Emmy stands to the side, smiling and watching the door of the neighbouring theatre out of the corner of her eye. *Come on, Mrs. Williams, now is the time*, she thinks.

Sensing that she needs to draw his attention more, Alice places a hand on his arm and gently guides him to turn with her, away from the door Mrs. Williams is waiting behind.

"See right there, on the corner there," Alice points. "The Queen's Hare, that is the place if you ever want to find me after a show, that is where I will be."

Emmy can see that the detective is struggling now that Alice has turned him. He wants to turn back to look at the stage door, to keep doing his duty, but he is intrigued by Alice and wants to give her his attention as well. Mrs. Williams needs to move now.

The door opens tentatively and Mrs. Williams, looking like nothing more than a washer woman, emerges from the theatre and walks down the street away from Alice and Emmy. Emmy gives a signal to Alice that they are in the clear and to finish up.

"It was so nice to meet you. You make sure to drop in sometime and see me." Alice pats his cheek as a finale and takes Emmy's arm again.

They walk out to the main street and make their way to a taxi stand. Emmy sees Colin run behind the theatre and then a few minutes later emerge without the detective in pursuit. He gestures for the uniformed men to follow and they all take the cab behind the one Emmy and Alice get in.

"It worked, they are leaving the detective to wait for Georgia Ann, who your doorman will confirm is still in the building and that it is typical for her to stay this long.

Mrs. Williams is away and should be making her way to the station. We will draw the attention to Gwen's house, which will be quite the flow of people."

"Then what, Emmy?"

"Then I need to sneak out of Gwen's and meet up with Mrs. Williams at the station. Make sure she gets on the train."

CHAPTER 14

July 19, 1913

THE PARTY IS LAVISH beyond words. Crystal champagne flutes and sculptures made of ice greet Emmy and Alice when they enter. Hordes of white roses decorate the rooms and every space is covered in luxury and opulence. Gwen is the main feature of any room she is in, however. Her dress is as stunning as any wedding gown she may be planning on wearing. The cream-coloured lace that runs over the bodice and down the three-quarter-length sleeves highlights the pale mauve chiffon that sits beneath it. It gathers at the waist with a cream satin belt and a large brooch of diamonds and brilliant sapphires. The dress cascades elegantly to the floor in tiers of mauve and lace that slowly transform into a blue that reflects the sapphires. Around her neck hangs a necklace of delicate pearls in three strands, drawing attention to her décolletage. Her hair is bound up in curls, neatly but voluminously tucked in seamless loops, with a diamond tiara shining through.

"Emmy, Miss Sinclair, how lovely to see you," Gwen rushes to them and kisses each cheek before saying another word.

"You look beautiful," Emmy says, feeling relieved that they took the time to change.

"Wait until you see my wedding dress," Gwen winks and turns to offer them a glass of champagne from a footman standing next to her.

"Thank you for allowing me to join Emmy," Alice adds.

"Of course, I wouldn't have been happy unless you two were here." Gwen takes Alice's hands as if they were old friends and not new acquaintances.

"Gwen, you are a saint. Now, I need to speak with you in private." Emmy's face conveys the seriousness of the situation.

"Follow me." Gwen glides through the crowd, politely nodding at people as she passes. She leads Emmy to a small serving pantry off the dining room, where Emmy explains the situation and the plan.

"Oh dear," Gwen says when Emmy is finished. "You do need my help. Don't worry, Miss Sinclair and I will hold the fort here and you can sneak out the back door, just this way."

Through the kitchen, and down the stairs, Gwen guides them to the servants' entrance in the back. "Emmy, do be careful, Colin is likely covering the back entrance. You know how he is."

"I know, that is why I must go right away. He was only just behind us, so hopefully I have beat him to the chase. Alice will stay here with you."

"Be safe," they both whisper as Emmy leaves.

Emmy slips out the back door and hurries through to the street. She does not spot Colin or any other police yet. She has made it in time. Turning south, she begins her trek to the station and away from the lavish party. The rain begins to drizzle and Emmy quickens her pace, not wanting to ruin Alice's dress. She will have to take the Underground in order to make it on time.

When Colin left the theatre, he had taken a gamble on Emmy's next move and had gone straight to the train station. When only two women came out of the theatre, he knew something was up. Sure, Georgia Ann Greenwood was known to stay late working in her office, but why was Mrs. Williams not making an attempt to get on the train to Southampton when her boat was leaving today? Why was her husband still planning on travelling to Canada, without her? Something in his gut had made him convince Marlowe, in his telegram earlier, to send a whole squad of constables to the train station to wait for Mrs. Williams. They were stationed at each car and were examining every person who tried to board.

When Emmy arrives on the scene, the light drizzle has managed to soak her through to the bone. She shudders in the cold and then again at the sight of all the uniformed officers she sees in the chaos of the station. Two at each train car checking everyone's documents.

"Bugger," Emmy swears as she scans for Mrs. Williams. This is really going to test the quality of her forged documents and disguises, not to mention Mrs. Williams' acting chops. Walking into the crowd of people, Emmy heads to the third-class area of the platform. She sees Mr. Williams as she goes, making his way to the first-class car with several porters carrying his luggage.

When she gets to third class, Emmy cannot see Mrs. Williams at all. She weaves her way through people, families, trunks, children running, and finally, after several minutes of panic, sees what she thinks is Mrs. Williams' hat.

"Vera, Vera Gilbert, is that you?" she calls out and Mrs. Williams turns around. Good sign.

"Miss Nation, how good to see you." Her eyes show a look of panic reflecting Emmy's own. Her calm demeanour from earlier having vanished at the sight of the police.

"It is indeed." Emmy takes her in a hug and whispers in her ear, "You will be fine. Trust the documents and trust your disguise. You know who you are, and you will make it past these silly coppers. I am sure of it."

"Yes, of course." Mrs. Williams nods her head resolutely. "Well, I'm off. I will try to find your mother as soon as I get on the boat."

Emmy watches as Mrs. Williams climbs the stairs into one of the many third-class train cars and comes face to face with two large and, hopefully, dim-witted police constables.

"Ticket and identification," the first barks at her. Mrs. Williams passes over her ticket and the fake identification documents General Drummond had provided in the name of Vera Gilbert. The constable stares at her papers for a long moment, while the second officer compares the woman in front of him to the likeness of Mrs. Williams.

"Take your hat off," he demands, and Mrs. Williams obliges.

"Looks kind of like our girl, doesn't it?" He turns back to check with his partner.

"A bit older, but I see the resemblance."

"What are you doing going to Southampton and where'd you get the money?"

"I'm going home," Mrs. Williams says in her most Canadian accent. "I just came to England to bury my sister who lived here. My employer was gracious enough to pay for the fare and for my ticket for the boat leaving this afternoon."

"She can't be Mrs. Williams, she doesn't talk like a well-to-do lady."

"But, look at the picture." The constable holds up a picture of Mrs. Williams next to her face. The two officers stare for an extended moment of silence.

"I don't know any Mrs. Williams," Mrs. Williams finally fills the space. "I have a second cousin named Martha Willis, maybe you are looking for her. I've never met her, but perhaps we have a family resemblance."

"Let's call over Officer Thomas. Let him decide."

The conductor blows his whistle, yelling "All aboard!" in his booming voice.

"We have to get on this train," someone from behind Mrs. Williams yells. She turns to see a crowd of passengers waiting behind her. "We've got tickets," another voice adds. "Let us on."

"I'm not sure. I see similarities, but she does look older and her hair is the wrong colour." The constables regroup. "We don't want to start a riot."

"Fine, fine, go on through."

Mrs. Williams nods her head slightly and quietly goes through their security checkpoint. She makes her way to an open seat and settles in with her bag on her knees, where she will be Vera Gilbert until she arrives in Southampton. From there, the local suffragettes will get her to the boat where her Vera Gilbert disguise will hopefully work a second time and get her into a cabin in third class. Once the boat has cleared any chance of Scotland Yard stopping it, she will put aside her disguise and slip upstairs to her husband and Mrs. Nation in first class.

When Emmy sees Mrs. Williams pass through the two constables, she breathes a sigh of relief. But when she turns to leave, she sees Colin directing a group of officers a little farther down the platform. Her heart drops. Why wasn't Colin waiting outside Gwen's house for her? That is what he does, he waits for her and makes sure no trouble comes her way. Why was he here and not there?

"Bugger," Emmy whispers. Colin had out-thought her, had been one step ahead, and had never followed her to Gwen's party. He must have known all along that she would end up at the station with Mrs. Williams. Obviously, his trust in her was gone.

She should wait to see the train get away without Mrs. Williams being apprehended, but she cannot risk being discovered, and the uniformed constables are pouring into the crowd faster and faster. Emmy lowers her head and walks towards the street. By the time she makes her way out of the chaos of people, she knows what she has to do. She turns back and scans the faces until she spots Colin. She looks at him for a long time, for the last time. He is beautiful and she loves him. Despite all they've been through, she loves him.

Emmy turns her back to him when the tears start to pool in her eyes. She must walk, one foot first, then the other, and get away. Her heart makes her body resist the commands her brain is giving, but she fights her way to the end of the platform and when she turns the corner, everything seems a little easier. She can no longer look back and see him, she can only look forward, to what she must do.

She runs now, all the way to Mrs. Pankhurst's office, and bursts through the front door.

"Mrs. Pankhurst? Mrs. Pankhurst?" she calls out, catching her breath and feeling sweat run down her back.

"We are in here, Emmy," the familiar voice responds. "What is the matter, did Mrs. Williams not get away?" Emmy comes tumbling into the room with her hat in her hand and wind-blown hair.

"I am not sure. The whole plan was spoiled, the police knew what we were up to. Mrs. Williams got on the train, she fooled the constables on guard, but I had to leave before the train departed. The police were everywhere, and Colin. Colin knew, he didn't wait for me, he knew what I was going to do, and he beat me there. And I've left Alice at Gwen's engagement party. I told her I would come back, but I didn't. I ran straight here. We need to tell her—the police will still be waiting outside Gwen's house for her to leave. She needs to be warned. Who knows what they have planned for her?" Emmy erupts in a flurry of tears and panic.

"Slow down. Flora, will you pour Emmy a cup of tea?" Mrs. Pankhurst sits Emmy down in an armchair in front of the fire.

"Oh, hello, Mrs. Drummond, I didn't see you there." Emmy looks up at Flora Drummond. "Thank you for sending Verna and Sheila, they were wonderful," Emmy manages to add, more calmly.

"You're welcome," she replies, handing Emmy a cup of tea. "Don't worry, I will get the message to Alice."

"Thank you," Emmy says between sips of tea. "I cannot go back home, I have to disappear. Colin, the police, I fear they have found me out. I need to leave Scotland Yard and Colin."

Mrs. Pankhurst and Mrs. Drummond look to each other with a twinkle in their eyes. Something had just fallen in their laps and they both knew it. Emmy was the solution to a major problem.

"All right, dear," Mrs. Pankhurst says. "We understand and we will help you. In fact, we have a mission for you, should you wish to take it on. It will be quite dangerous."

"What is it?"

"We cannot keep going the way we are, hiding and disguising women. We need more to protect them, to protect us. The disguises are wonderful and we should continue that practice, and your mother's hospice in the country has been a safe haven for so many women, but we need an army. I still need to be making public appearances, as do our other speakers and leaders, but we simply cannot do it with the Cat and Mouse Act in place. We cannot get rearrested every time we go outside. Emmy, you have done an amazing job at hiding women and getting them safely out of London, but we cannot leave London. We have to stay and we have to fight, publicly."

"What do you propose?" Emmy asks, unsure what this all means.

"We need a bodyguard."

"A bodyguard? Of women? Against the police?" Emmy can hardly contain her laughter at such a preposterous idea, but Mrs. Drummond and Mrs. Pankhurst are staring back at her in all sincerity.

"Yes," Mrs. Drummond declares simply.

"Yes," Mrs. Pankhurst adds more softly. "We need a bodyguard of women, who are trained to defend themselves against the brutalities of the police and protect speakers from being arrested on the stage."

Emmy takes a breath to overcome her laughter before she speaks again.

"You want women to fight the Metropolitan Police Force? You want them to train in combat techniques and stand up against armed men?"

"I know it sounds crazy, but look at you," Mrs. Pankhurst implores. "You've taken down a few constables lately. With Marion Campbell, for example. You could help us with this. We've already got Edith Garrud on board to train the women in jujitsu and Gertrude Harding to organize it all. But, Emmy, we need your intelligence on Scotland Yard, and your help training and organizing the Bodyguard around how the police train and organize themselves. Do you see?"

"I do. I think it sounds a bit far-fetched, but I do see."

"Will you help us?"

"I am not sure that we will be able to shape a group of suffragettes into a fighting army of guards, but I will help in any way I can."

"I knew you would." Mrs. Pankhurst smiles.

"You will have to go completely underground." General Drummond takes command. "It is too dangerous to stay at Scotland Yard, as you said, and we cannot run the risk of you being arrested yourself. Which means you have to disappear. I will figure out lodging for you. Go home now and pack all the things you need. Then go to this address," she hands Emmy a slip of paper.

"Tonight?"

"You must leave right away." Mrs. Pankhurst lays a gentle hand on her shoulder and leads her out the door.

Emmy tucks the address in her pocket and takes a deep breath. Then she runs all the way home.

CHAPTER 15

July 19, 1913

EDITH IS WAITING FOR her when she arrives at her flat. The first thing Emmy notices is how sad she looks.

"Emmy?" she almost whispers it. "Please?" Emmy knows what Edith wants. She wants Emmy to stop and hear her out. She wants to explain, to be forgiven, to be friends again.

Part of Emmy boils up. Edith betrayed her and her mother, and she could have compromised her position inside Scotland Yard. But, who is Emmy to judge someone for betraying her friends? It was Emmy's betrayal that had Edith arrested and tortured in Holloway, and Edith had forgiven Emmy for that.

"Edith, you don't need to say anything." Emmy takes her friend's hand in hers, and the soft kid leather of Edith's delicate gloves remind Emmy of their first day selling newspapers together. "You are my friend and you did what you needed to do to get your children back. I do not need any explanation or apology. We have all done things that we are not proud of, but we are here and we are together and we will support each other, no matter what."

Edith bursts into tears and wraps Emmy in an embrace. Emmy is gripped with a fierceness that does not conceal the trembling of Edith's sobs. She holds her friend, tenderly, until Edith has calmed down enough to speak.

"Oh, Emmy, I was so worried. I was so scared to see you," Edith snivels into Emmy's shoulder.

"I was scared to see you, too, after you discovered my secret. Edith, I understand what you have been through and I understand why you would take the police up on their offer. You did what you needed to do."

"I did. I need my children more than I need my freedom. Do you understand?"

"Yes, I do. How about a cup of tea and you can tell me everything that little John and Inez have gotten up to," Emmy suggests.

The pair walk hand in hand up to Emmy's flat, where they talk for the next hour about everything that has happened since their parting. Even though Colin might walk in at any moment to arrest her, Emmy allows herself this time with Edith because she knows it will be the last time she sees her friend. This will be their goodbye. By the end, the betrayals are forgotten on both sides, as only the truest friendships will allow.

"Are you coming back to the WSPU?" Emmy asks.

"No, I don't think that I will. It would be too hard now to deceive John. He is having me watched like a hawk at all times. Even now, the chauffeur has been sitting outside in the motor car the whole time we've been in here. I am sure to get an earful when John gets his report this evening. Besides, I am no longer useful to Scotland Yard since I've been discovered."

"Oh, Edith, that sounds terrible. How can you stand it?"

"Because I get to wake up every morning and see the beautiful faces of John Jr. and Inez. Mostly I don't leave my house unless I am with them. I thought of writing you a letter instead of coming in person, but I needed to see you, I needed my friend."

"You have me," Emmy reaches out and takes her friend's hand again. "You will always have me. Even if I am not with you." Emmy fights the tears forming in her eyes.

After Edith leaves Emmy alone in her flat, she takes her carpet bag from her closet and throws in as many clothes as she can fit. She has the clothes that Gwen bought her when she got promoted, a few mementoes from her childhood home, and some things from Mrs. Lawrence's. She takes the small portrait she has of her mother and father together, and a book that Colin had given her. Lastly, she takes the candle snuffer that her mother used when Emmy was a child, and the iron fire poker that belonged to Mrs. Lawrence. She leaves all the clothes, jewels, and gifts Cliff had given her, neatly packed in the closet.

Emmy looks around the tiny flat that was her first home all to herself. This was where she discovered true independence and freedom. This is where she fell in love. This was more her home than any of the other houses she had lived in. It feels empty now, hollow, even though all the furniture, dishes, and paintings on the wall are still in place. They were there when she moved in, but the place had seemed full then. Full of life and hope. Now, these objects loom like ghosts in the shadows, haunting her choices. Edith and Colin cannot follow her on this next stage of her journey. She must go alone and leave without a trace.

But, surely a note would be okay? In fact, if she did disappear without a trace, Colin would certainly come looking for her, thinking something had happened and not that she had left voluntarily. She had to let him know not to follow, not to search, not to worry. But what to say?

A few agonizing minutes later, she seals the envelope and places it on the table, along with her keys. Then she swings the bag over her shoulder like a messenger would, so she has both arms free, and turns back to take a final look at the tiny London flat that was all her own. The iron fire poker sticks out the top of the bag like a flagpole without a flag.

"Goodbye," she says to the empty space that is still filled with all the furniture it came with, but is now missing everything that made it a home. The curtains are drawn, the bed is made, and the chairs are all tucked in neatly. She had washed all the dishes and left the ones she had brought with her. She wouldn't need them where she was going.

Emmy closes the door on that life. She forces herself not to look back as she goes down the stairs and out the front door of the building.

With her bag on her back, Emmy swings her bicycle out of the alleyway, where it lived for a long time, and into the street. She climbs up and starts to pedal. She succeeds in not turning back to look, but she cannot suppress the tears that slowly begin to roll down her cheeks.

She rides all the way to the address Flora had given her, with the wind in her hair and her mind elsewhere. She thinks about what Mrs. Pankhurst and General Drummond just asked of her. To help create a bodyguard of women to defend them against Scotland Yard, to go up against a trained battalion of men in hand-to-hand combat. It sounds like a crazy idea, but Emmy can also see the need for it. These women though, they will be committing assault against officers of the Met, and even with the best training, they could not possibly hope to win against a whole unit. So, they would be putting themselves in harm's way and risk being arrested, in order to protect the leaders of the WSPU. Not quite a suicide mission, but most certainly a sacrificial-lamb mission. Of course, Emmy would help. She could not sit back and let her fellow suffragettes get beaten without at least giving her support in their training. But it also means leaving Colin for an indefinite period of time.

"This is not forever," she says to the wind. "One day, we will be given the vote and all of this will go away and I will come home and be with Colin, and live a happy, peaceful life." It was more of a wish than a statement of fact. Emmy was starting to lose hope that the government would ever grant women the right to vote, or any other rights, for that matter.

By the time her bicycle pulls up outside the dojo where Edith Garrud and Gertrude Harding are waiting for her, Emmy's face is tear-streaked and her eyes red-rimmed.

Her bike ride had cleared her head. It was not the fact that she was leaving another home that was making her sad. It wasn't leaving Scotland Yard, or Cliff, or any of that life that she had before. It was Colin. Leaving Colin was going to be the hardest thing she had ever done. Harder than leaving her parents' house and arriving in London with nothing but an address. Harder than learning a new skill and going out in a workforce that she had never had any experience with. It was going to be harder than going undercover and lying to everyone who meant something to her. As she rode away from the home that was all her own, but also a home with Colin, she realized just how much he meant to her. He was more than a flutter in her stomach. He was more than her best friend and closest confidant. He was more than a rush of blood to her cheeks when he touched her. He was the love of her life, and she had to leave him behind.

❦

Colin arrives home that evening, exhausted. It had been a challenging day. He had suspected Emmy of helping Mrs. Williams escape and he had been wrong. Mrs. Williams was still in her house, sick from the imprisonment, and Mr. Williams had gone on without her to fulfill the speaking engagement on her behalf. Emmy and Alice Sinclair had been at Gwen's party all evening, and Georgia Ann Greenwood had stayed locked in her office at the theatre. All of this was confirmed, and the boat had left Southampton with no trace of Mrs. Williams at the pier. He had been wrong to doubt Emmy, and he felt as gloomy about it as the sky looked with all the rain clouds hanging overhead, waiting to let loose their watery innards.

He decides to give it a bit of time before he knocks on Emmy's door. He would have to apologize, even though she couldn't possibly know that he had betrayed her again. He had to come clean because she was Emmy and he respected her and wanted her trust, always. But first, he has to get cleaned up. He runs a bath, eager to relax his sore muscles for a few minutes before owning up to his actions.

Half an hour later, he is warm, clean, and dressed in dry clothing to knock on the adjoining door between the two flats. There is no answer, but Emmy's door creaks open. She had left it unlocked. She never leaves it unlocked. Walking in, Colin immediately senses her absence, even though everything is still in place. The furniture is where it should be, the dishes are stacked in their normal places, the paintings are still hanging on the walls. Yet, something is off. He notices a note on the table and walks towards it. His name is on the envelope and his heart sinks. He runs to the closet, rips open the door, and sees the emptiness. Only the gifts from Cliff are left hanging like shadows of what once lived here. She is gone. Emmy Nation is gone. She has left him behind. He tears open the envelope and sinks to the floor as he reads.

Dearest Colin,

I am sorry to leave without warning or saying goodbye. The thought of it was too difficult to bear. This way seemed easier, however, now that I am writing this letter, I am not sure that it is.

I am leaving the flat and the Metropolitan Police Force. I cannot tell you where I am going, or for how long I will be gone. Please do not look for me. I know you will be inclined to ignore this request, but I beg you to honour it. What I must go do, must be done without your help.

You have protected me well and have been a loyal ally in the midst of a chaotic world. I am deeply grateful to have had the past few months with you. Working side by side with you brought me my most cherished memories. I will never forget your kindness and encouragement in my first assignment as an undercover agent. Do you remember our first night together? It still brings a smile to my face. We were so shy and uncomfortable with each other, I would never have guessed that we would grow to be... well, you know.

Promise me you will not come looking for me and that you will forgive me for leaving like this, without a word.

I will come back. I do not know when, but one day, I will come back and I will want to hear about all of your adventures. So, don't forget a single one.

Love,

Emmy

P.S. I know I have no right to ask this, but since I won't be here to know your answer or be embarrassed, I will be bold and go out on a limb. It would be lovely if you did not fall in love and get married while I am away. Now I am blushing writing this and wish I could tear the paper. Please disregard this. Fall in love with whomever you wish, but know that I will be sad to hear of it. Bugger, I did it again, wrote more than I wish I had. I am actually leaving now, although it pains me greatly. Goodbye, Colin.

Colin sits in the middle of the floor in Emmy's flat and reads the letter over and over again, particularly the last part, the postscript. How is he supposed to let her walk out of his life after she says that? But after the initial shock and sadness, a smile creeps across Colin's face. Emmy has finally embraced it, she has realized her true allegiance is not to Scotland Yard and Clifford Marlowe, but to the women's fight. He is proud and happy and excited for her. He knows this is where she truly belongs, and now she has gone to them completely. It is what is right, and hopefully, when they have achieved their goal, she will come home to him and he will be waiting for her. Always, waiting.

Emmy carries her bag through the hallway. She sees the door at the end with the outline of where a sign used to be. As she gets closer, she hears the odd sounds that are coming from behind it. Grunts and thumps roll consistently out, and Emmy wonders what the people who reside upstairs are thinking about all of this.

She leaves her heavy bag in the hall and slowly turns the handle. Standing in the doorway, her eyes take a few moments to adjust to the bright electric lights hanging from the ceiling.

Emmy steps into a large gymnasium-style room, with mats spread out all over the floor, wall to wall. Familiar-looking equipment rests on shelves along one wall and the all-too-present smell of sweat comes her way. The room is filled with ladies, all fighting each other. A tiny woman, no taller than a twelve-year-old, walks amongst them as they fight. Emmy recognizes her. It is Edith Garrud.

"You are strong," Mrs. Garrud yells out to the fighters. "You are tough. You don't take any guff from anyone. You are fighters. You fight for your rights. You are Amazons. You are Amazons," she champions them all on.

Emmy watches as the women toss each other to the floor and then help each other back up. Some of the women wear just their petticoats and blouses, while others have changed into bloomers. They struggle, wrestle, throw each other around, and then help each other regain their balance before starting all over again.

"Miss Nation?" A soft voice grabs Emmy's attention.

"Yes, that is me," Emmy replies, turning around to see a sweet-faced young woman that Emmy remembers from Emily Wilding Davison's funeral.

"Oh, good. We've been waiting for you. I'm Gert, Gert Harding, and that is Edith Garrud." Gert points to the tiny figure weaving in and out of the fighters. "It is a pleasure to meet you again. Welcome to the home of the Amazons. Welcome to the Bodyguard."

· EPILOGUE ·

THE CHURCH BELLS CHIME for midnight and a small figure crouches in the shadows created by the moon against
the towering stone buildings of London. When the bells
fall still, the silence of the city street returns like a fog set-
tling, only to be broken by the spatter of heavy boots on
stone. The police constables run by, confused and lost.

"She couldn't have gone this far. We weren't that far
behind her," one says to the other, slowing down and
leaning over with his hands on his knees.

"She's small and fast. Don't underestimate her," the
other replies between deep breaths.

Don't underestimate her, indeed, she chuckles to herself.

"You go ahead. I am going to look around here."

"I'm telling you, she's gone. Long gone."

"Well, I'm staying."

"Suit yourself," he replies and continues running.
With him out of the way, she sees the alleyway beyond the
open street. A safer haven and maybe a safe passage, too.
But one constable had stayed behind.

She moves quickly, like a ghost that rests at the corner
of your eye, but never fully comes into view. The ankles

of the constable feel her presence first, as she gracefully swings one of her legs into the back of them, using her other leg as a pivot point. The power of the swing knocks him to the ground with a crunch and a thud. As soon as he lands, her elbow finds the softness of his overripe mid-section, pushing the air up and out of his lungs in a quiet huff. Then she pirouettes up to her feet, bringing a foot down hard on his forearm. She covers his mouth with one hand, indicating for him to be silent with a finger over her lips. Then she grabs his free arm in hers and silently twists it until it is near to snapping out of its socket. His eyes fill with terror and pain, but he doesn't make a sound.

She bends low to his ear and whispers, "Do not follow me, or I will do much worse. Tell your friends at the Yard, the Bodyguard has arrived in London. We wish you no harm, but we will no longer let our sister suffragettes be hurt at your hands." She releases him and disappears into the shadows of the alley, turning back to ensure the constable is doing as she instructed before she climbs over the fence and vanishes into the night.

Author's Notes

WHILE WRITING THIS BOOK, I was constantly walking the line of fiction or history, as I'm sure all historical novelists do. When is it acceptable to bend history to suit the needs of the story, and when do the needs of the story need to take second place to the facts of history? This is a hard call to make, and I hope that I have made the right choices in this book. But, what I hope the most is that the fictional story of Emmy Nation will inspire you, the reader, to do your own research. I hope that Emmy's story makes you curious enough to pick up a biography or a history book to read the true stories of the many women who fought for the rights we have today. Their stories are just like Emmy's, filled with moral questioning, difficult relationships with the men in their lives, and yes, in some cases, action. I encourage you, in particular, to look into Gertrude Harding, Edith Garrud, and Emily Wilding Davison, among the other women whose lives inspired this book and are featured: the Pankhurst family, Annie Kenney, Flora Drummond, Sophia Duleep Singh, Cicely Hamilton, and Harriet Kerr.

Acknowledgments

THIS BOOK HAS GONE through many ups and downs, but it has made it here to the page because of the unwavering support of my husband, Steve. Thank you for talking about Emmy whenever I needed, encouraging me to keep going when things felt too overwhelming, and always being my biggest fan.

I am also deeply grateful to Chris Kay Fraser, Britt Smith, the Firefly Creative Writing team, and Sarah MacKinnon for helping me shape this idea into a story worth sharing.

Of course, I wouldn't have bothered finishing this book if it weren't for the support of my family, friends, and the readers of Emmy Nation. Your connection to these characters inspired me to keep writing.

A million thank yous.

Historical Notes

Chapter 1 - Interpretations of the Cat and Mouse Act are inspired from *My Own Story* by Emmeline Pankhurst.

Chapter 2 - Inspiration for the actresses and the theatre, as well as details of the Actresses' Franchise League, come from biographies of Cicely Hamilton and Edith Craig, amongst others.

Chapter 5 - Representations of Cicely Hamilton, Edith Craig, Christabel Marshall, and Sophia Duleep Singh are inspired by their biographies. More on the Women Writers' Suffrage League and the Women's Tax Resistance League can be discovered in the biography of Cicely Hamilton. The play, *How the Vote Was Won*, is from Cicely Hamilton's large body of work as a writer.

Chapter 7 - Details of Emily Wilding Davison's death and her funeral are inspired from *With All Her Might* by Gretchen Wilson, *My Own Story* by Emmeline Pankhurst, and *Emily Wilding Davison: A Suffragette's Family Album* by Maureen Howes. The involvement of the Actresses' Franchise League and Edith Garrud was added for the purposes of the story.

Chapter 14 and 15 - Details of the Bodyguard are inspired from *With All Her Might* by Gretchen Wilson.

Selected Bibliography

Anand, Anita. *Sophia: Princess, Suffragette, Revolutionary*. New York: Bloomsbury, 2015.

Cockin, Katharine. *Edith Craig and the Theatres of Art*. London: Bloomsbury Methuen Drama, an imprint of Bloomsbury Publishing Plc, 2017.

Howes, Maureen. *Emily Wilding Davison: A Suffragette's Family Album*. Gloucestershire: The History Press, 2013.

Pankhurst, Emmeline. *My Own Story*. London: Eveleigh Nash, 1914.

Whitelaw, Lis. *The Life and Rebellious Times of Cicely Hamilton: Actress, Writer, Suffragist*. London: Women's Press, 1990.

Wilson, Gretchen. *With All Her Might: The Life of Gertrude Harding Militant Suffragette*. New Brunswick: Goose Lane Editions, 1996.

About the Author

L. DAVIS MUNRO HOLDS a Masters of Arts in Drama from York University with a focus on the theatre of the women's suffrage movement and has worked as a dramaturge, director, and producer in the dance and theatre scene in Toronto since 2012. Her debut novel, *Emmy Nation: Undercover Suffratte*, was published in 2015. This is her second novel.

LDavisMunro.com

43935766R00175

Made in the USA
Lexington, KY
04 July 2019